Ghostly
Tales of
Pennsylvania

Dedication:
To Landon, Logan, Ella, Brielle, Avery, Luke, and Isabelle. Thank you for supporting us while we stuck our faces in our laptops to research and write, and for listening to us obsess about haunted prisons, state hospitals, Civil War field hospitals, and book deadlines.

To our Ghost Stories Ink brothers: Shawn McCann and Sean Spinks, with special acknowledgments to Scott Hendricks, Kevin Swanson, and Kerry Peterson. You chase inspiration with us through haunted buildings, and you are as nerdy about all things creepy as we are. You make our weirdness seem normal(ish).

In some instances, names and locations have been changed at the request of sources.

Content Warning: This book contains retellings of historical events. Some tales include references to suicide, murder, and torture and may not be appropriate for all audiences.

Cover design by Jonathan Norberg
Text design by Karla Linder
Edited by Andrew Mollenkof
Proofread by Emily Beaumont

All images copyrighted.
Images used under license from Shutterstock.com:
Covers and silhouettes: **jenesesimre:** vulture; **ViLannon:** branches

10 9 8 7 6 5 4 3 2 1
Ghostly Tales of Pennsylvania
Copyright © 2024 by Jessica Freeburg and Natalie Fowler
Published by Adventure Publications
An imprint of AdventureKEEN
310 Garfield Street South
Cambridge, Minnesota 55008
(800) 678-7006
www.adventurepublications.net
All rights reserved
Printed in the U.S.A.
Cataloging-in-Publication data is available from the
Library of Congress
ISBN 978-1-64755-468-2 (pbk.); ISBN 978-1-64755-469-9 (ebook)

Ghostly Tales of Pennsylvania

Jessica Freeburg and **Natalie Fowler**

PUBLICATIONS
Adventure

Table of Contents

Acknowledgments

The authors would like to thank several people who made this book possible.

We want to start by thanking the amazing team at AdventureKEEN for giving our stories a home. We'd also like to thank Liliane Opsomer for years of marketing and media-relations support and for always being a delight to work with. We feel so blessed by the partnership we have with the entire team at AdventureKEEN, and we want you all to know how much we value and appreciate each of you!

We would also like to thank all the paranormal investigators out there who have done such a great job of documenting paranormal activity through television shows, articles, books, blogs, and podcasts. All of your work contributes to answering common questions the general public may have and inspires us as we search for understanding about what makes a place haunted and what we are interacting with on an investigation.

Finally, to our book-loving, think-outside-the-box agent, Dawn Frederick—thank you for your endless support. You are more than a business partner; you are a soul sister, and we love you.

Preface

Pennsylvania is a state rich in history, founded by William Penn in 1681, after King Charles II granted Penn land rights to build a colony. Penn was a vocal member and supporter of the Quaker religious group, whose constituents were persecuted in England for their beliefs that all men and women were equally connected to God. This idea fundamentally contradicted the orthodox religious beliefs of a society devoted to the hierarchy of kings and queens. Penn envisioned a peaceful, safe place for Quakers to live in the New World.

Experts believe that Indigenous Peoples—including the Erie, Iroquois (Seneca and Oneida), Lenape, Munsee, Shawnee, and Susquehannock tribes—inhabited the area for tens of thousands of years before Europeans colonized it. One can imagine the countless individuals, with all of their joys and sorrows, leaving their marks on the fabric of the region. Whispers of their past echo across the plains, deep into the valleys, and through the peaks of the Appalachian Mountains.

From the crumbling walls of the historic Eastern State Penitentiary—where more than 85,000 convicted criminals, including infamous mob boss Al Capone, served their sentences—to the hallowed battlefields of Gettysburg, the imprints of the past reverberate into the present. We can only wonder why—or how. Are some spirits trapped, destined to replay the tragedy of their deaths for centuries to come? Does the collective fear felt by hundreds of young men charging into battle leave a stain that time cannot erase? Do some souls simply return to places that filled their hearts with happiness during their lifetimes, becoming eternal caretakers of locations they once loved?

Whatever the cause, it is difficult to ignore the enduring connection between spirits and the landscapes of the lives they once led. It seems as if the veil between the living and the dead might be more of a wisp than a cloak. At the heart of this collection of ghostly tales, the past covers the present like a thick fog, sweeping across a field where the soil once ran red with the blood of war.

Eastern State Penitentiary
Philadelphia

Some locations hold trauma like a jar with its lid twisted on too tightly. No matter how hard one tries, they can never empty the contents. Eastern State Penitentiary is an example of such a place. Home to thousands of convicted criminals, this vessel contains memories so dark and haunting that shadows don't bother hiding in the corners. They are right at home, moving freely among the rays of sun that stream through the skylights above. It seems that those who were silenced in the past refuse to remain quiet in the present.

* * *

In early colonial America, the authorities designed prisons for mass incarceration. Men, women, and children were housed together in large, communal cells. A hungry child jailed for stealing a loaf of bread was locked away with murderers and rapists. Prisons were filthy breeding grounds for disease, assault, and robbery.

When prison reformers called for more humane punishment of criminals in the late 1700s, Pennsylvania, a colony rooted in the Quaker faith, became the home of the world's first true penitentiary. The term "penitentiary" comes from the idea that criminals should make penance for their sins. The institution was inspired by the Quakers' belief that true reformation comes through repentance, brought about in the quiet contemplation found in solitary confinement.

Construction of the Eastern State Penitentiary began in 1822. Built on 10 acres of farmland known as Cherry Hill, the facility was initially called Cherry Hill State Prison. With high-arching ceilings, glass skylights, and gothic architecture, the building gave off the air of a house of worship rather than a home of reform for criminals. That sense of religious nostalgia was, by design, meant to inspire repentance.

The prison welcomed its first inmate, Charles Williams, a farmer found guilty of thievery, in October 1829. He was led into the facility with a hood over his face, and his two years of isolation began.

Prisoners at the penitentiary would spend 23 hours a day in one of the facility's 8x12x10-foot concrete cells. They were allowed one to two daily exercise breaks outdoors in a private yard. Cells were essentially impervious to outside noise, leaving prisoners with only the sounds of their own thoughts. Inmates were provided three meals a day, a Bible to read, and work to complete in their cells, such as weaving or shoemaking. The goal was complete isolation.

While the idea of solitude and self-reflection was rooted in compassion and carried the intention of moving criminals toward true repentance and a better life, many critics argued that the reality was torturous. They believed the isolation led to insanity and even death, rather than reform.

Enforcing such strict isolation meant punishing those who broke the rules. This led to a number of public scandals. The first came just four years after the penitentiary opened. Prisoner Mathias Maccumsey died after being punished with an iron gag for speaking to another inmate. This torture device was essentially a piece of metal pushed into the victim's mouth and attached to their wrists, which were handcuffed behind their back. Any movement or attempts to speak caused the tongue to tear. Maccumsey's official cause of death was "apoplexy," or unconsciousness resulting from a stroke or cerebral hemorrhage.

This was just one example of the extreme punishments to which inmates were subjected. During cold winter months, prisoners were submerged in a water bath. After being dunked in the water, they were chained to the wall and left to hang overnight as ice formed on their skin. Others were strapped into what was known as the "mad chair" and left there for days. Some were strapped in so tightly that their limbs later had to be amputated due to lack of circulation.

As if being isolated in one's room for 23 hours a day wasn't bad enough, guards would place inmates deemed unruly in "the Hole." These four tiny cells were devoid of light and plumbing. With limited circulation, the air was stifling, dank, and thick with the stench of urine and feces.

The "Death" book, still housed at the penitentiary, holds the names, dates, and manners of death of hundreds of inmates. Death by suicide was common, as were murder and illness. An epidemic of tuberculosis killed nearly 600 individuals at the penitentiary. Over the years, many inmates serving life sentences simply died of natural causes brought on by old age.

At least two guards lost their lives to violence, including overseer Michael T. Doran, who was murdered by inmate Joseph Taylor in 1834. No stranger to violence, Taylor was serving time for what the newspapers called "murderous assault." In addition to his general inclination toward violence, Taylor became convinced the guards were trying to poison him. On May 21, he disassembled the sewing machine that he used as a stocking weaver and clubbed Officer Doran to death in his private exercise yard. After murdering Doran, Taylor returned to his cell, lay down on his bed, and took a nap.

Reports of insanity, brought on by total isolation, and the startling number of inmates ending their own lives left many questioning the humanity of the prison's methods. In 1913, an era of total isolation for all convicts came to an end. Prison officials created common spaces and began housing prisoners in pairs.

By 1926, Eastern State, which was initially intended to hold 250 inmates, held 1,700. Over the years, the structure grew from its original seven single-story cell blocks to include eight additional two-story cell blocks. As the prison adapted and grew, violence continued to flourish within its walls. Riots, murder, and suicide remained prevalent until the prison closed its doors in 1971. In its 142 years of operation, nearly

85,000 prisoners lived there. Hundreds, perhaps even thousands, died there.

Given the history of human suffering and death at Eastern State Penitentiary, it's no surprise that it is considered one of the most haunted locations in America. Reports of ghostly activity began decades before it shut down. In fact, inmates and guards reported hauntings as early as the 1920s.

* * *

"This way, Mr. Capone," the guard said as he led notorious gangster Al Capone down the corridor. The guard stopped, moved aside, and nodded toward a cell that Capone had been sentenced to call home for the next year.

Capone stepped inside and surveyed the space. A cabinet radio was positioned against one wall. Elegant paintings hung on another.

Capone stood atop an Oriental rug that centered the small room, and he nodded. "It's not the penthouse, but it'll do."

"It's as close to the penthouse as a guy can get in this joint. I'm just down the way, within earshot. Let me know if you need anything," the guard said before closing the cell door and heading back to his post.

It was 1929, and Al Capone had made a name for himself as an infamous bootlegger in Chicago. That May, while traveling from Atlantic City back to Illinois, he stopped in Philadelphia, where he was arrested for illegally carrying a firearm. Knowing his reputation and wanting to make an example of him, the Philadelphia courts gave him the maximum sentence of one year in prison. So here he was, at Eastern State Penitentiary, settling into his home away from home.

Capone wasn't thrilled to be there—but unlike the other inmates, he'd been given his own cell, which he was allowed to furnish with the finer things that made it feel a little more luxurious. And, so far, the guards had been respectful. Then again, most people approached Capone with a measure of respect reserved for those who had hitmen on their paybooks.

It had only been three months since the Saint Valentine's Day Massacre had shaken Chicago. It hadn't been proven, but most assumed that Capone had ordered the murder of seven associates of his rival George "Bugs" Moran. The assassins, disguised as police officers, ordered the men to line up against the wall of a garage, where they were executed. One of those men was Bugs's brother-in-law, James Clark.

The murders put a target on Capone's back with law enforcement officials, who were tired of rampant gang violence terrorizing the nation. That crime would come back to haunt Capone . . . in more ways than one.

Capone turned on his radio and let the waltz fill his ears. He lay back on his bed and closed his eyes.

"Get away from me!" Capone's voice echoed off the brick walls throughout the cell block.

"No, Jimmy, leave me alone!" Capone yelled.

When a guard got to the cell, he braced himself for what he might find. How could another inmate have gotten into Capone's cell? He was ready for a fight to remove the offender. He knew that protecting Capone was the first step in protecting himself.

"Break it up," the guard yelled into the cell. But when he looked inside, he saw that there was nothing to break up.

Capone stood against the wall, his eyes wide, sweat dripping from his brow. "Did you see him?"

"See who?"

"Jimmy Clark."

The guard shook his head. "James Clark is dead, Mr. Capone."

"I know!" Capone's voice became quiet. "But he was here."

Al Capone stayed at Eastern State Penitentiary for eight months before being released. The ghost of James Clark reportedly haunted him on many of those nights. He was often heard begging Jimmy to leave him alone. According to legend, when Capone left the prison, he took Clark with him—and was haunted by his spirit for years to come.

* * *

By the 1940s, inmates and guards were reporting shadow figures and unexplained noises throughout the prison. Nowadays, the penitentiary is a historic site that offers tours and event rentals. Phantom voices and disembodied screams remain a common occurrence reported by staff and visitors. People also report being touched or pushed by unseen hands.

One tour guide recalled a startling experience in the rotunda—the center of the prison, where each cell block branches off. A person can stand in the center and look down each corridor to the very end.

On that particular day, the guide had just finished speaking with a group of about 40 visitors. As the group moved on, he noticed someone over his shoulder. Assuming a member of the tour was lagging, he turned to speak to him, but no one was there.

Again, he saw someone over his shoulder. And again, he turned to face him—but the rotunda was empty. That's when he saw the figure of a man moving slowly down a cell block. With each step, his image became more transparent until, eventually, the ghostly figure simply vanished.

Several paranormal television shows have filmed investigations at Eastern State Penitentiary. Their gathered evidence ranges from sounds of jail cells opening on their own and footsteps scuffling across the floor in empty cells to electronic voice phenomena, or EVPs (voices that were captured on recordings but were not heard by anyone present), calling investigators names and telling them to "get out." One team caught compelling footage of a black entity in the corridor of an empty cell block. The figure seemed to rise from the floor and rush back toward the end of the hallway.

Was a curious soul from the prison's dark history sneaking out of the shadows? Do the screams of past inmates, trapped in an eternal loop of suffering, slip into the present every now and then? It's hard to know for certain why some places seem to hold spiritual energy.

What we do know is that inmates entered Eastern State Penitentiary carrying the weight of their sins, whether they were remorseful or not. Others brought demons that wove a web in their minds like a venomous spider entangling its prey.

These walls are forever etched by the torture and madness of the criminals who were confined within them. Whether the shadows and voices that drift through the corridors are residual energy or intelligent spirits, there is no doubt: Eastern State Penitentiary is haunted by its past.

Old Jail Museum
Jim Thorpe

Built in 1871, the Carbon County Jail served Jim Thorpe and the surrounding Pennsylvania communities for nearly 125 years until it shut down in January of 1995. The McBride family purchased the building and turned it into the Old Jail Museum that we know it as today.

With a worn brick exterior, 3-foot-thick walls, and barred windows, the jail stands two stories high, with a tower rising out of the center. It is located on a raised plot of grass that is surrounded by a brick wall, topped with ornate iron fencing.

As was the case in many jails, the range of offenses for inmates was drastic. One man, in 1966, served a 9–18-month sentence—weekends only—for stealing a $38 lawn mower and a half case of cigarettes. Others served time for assault, robbery, and even murder. Some met their deaths at the end of the hangman's noose, which dangles from the wooden gallows within the Old Jail Museum.

One man who breathed his last breath at the end of that knotted rope was Alexander Campbell. An Irish coal miner, Campbell was convicted as a terroristic killer. In a plot straight out of a mystery novel, the famous Pinkerton Detective Agency sent one of their own undercover to find any coal miners who might be connected to the Molly Maguires, a secret society. Composed of Irishmen, the group was suspected of murder, arson, and violent assaults in an effort to fight against the deplorable working conditions inside the coal mines.

Although they denied involvement in the crimes, 20 Irish coal miners were hanged. On June 21, 1877, Campbell was among four who swung from the noose in the old jail. Their convictions were based on little more than the word of a Pinkerton detective. The other men who were executed that day included Michael Doyle, John Donohue, and Edward Kelly.

They would not be the last. More men were convicted as members of the Molly Maguires and died at the gallows inside the prison.

On March 28, 1878, Thomas P. Fisher was executed there. Ten months later, Charles Sharp and James McDonnell met the same fate. In all, seven of the 20 executed men—who many believed were innocent—paid with their lives at the Carbon County Jail.

The McBride family credited with turning the jail into a museum, felt compelled to preserve the building's connection to that fateful chain of events. The Irish coal miners, overworked and underpaid, wanted fair labor and compensation. Yet some of them were publicly killed for that dream.

Today, visitors can take a 30-minute guided tour of the jail, with proceeds going toward maintaining the historic structure.

* * *

The boy stood among a group of curious tourists just outside Cell 17.

The guide announced, "This is where Alexander Campbell spent his final days. Known in his community as a good husband and father, it's likely that his only crime was being an Irishman who believed the men working in the coal mines should be treated fairly. There has never been any evidence to suggest that he was part of a secret society that plotted to harm or kill anyone.

"Legend says that before he was led from this cell to the gallows, he placed his hand against the wall, high above his head, and proclaimed, 'As God is my witness, they are hanging an innocent man.' According to lore, Campbell also said, 'This handprint will remain as proof of my innocence.' It seems to have done exactly that," the guide concluded.

The boy peered curiously inside the cell before cautiously following his mother in to get a closer look. He stared in awe at the handprint, more than 140 years after Campbell had left it.

The guide added, "Despite every effort to remove the handprint, including repainting and replastering, it cannot be erased—much like the injustice committed against Campbell."

The boy had done a bit of research before visiting the old jail. He knew that some evidence suggested the handprint may have been left by Thomas P. Fisher, but legend often attributed it to Campbell. Whichever man left the mark, both carried the weight of the same tragic story. And one—or maybe both—seemed to have remained behind.

As the boy and his mother stood silently, looking up at the remnant of a life cut short, the temperature around them dropped.

"Do you feel that?" he asked his mother.

Her eyes widened, and she nodded. "It's suddenly freezing," she whispered.

The guide continued to speak from just outside the cell. "The last prisoner to be incarcerated in Cell 17 claimed that ghosts were terrorizing him, coming in and out of the cell. He screamed incessantly for hours, until he was finally moved to a different cell."

The hairs on the back of the boy's neck stood, and his flesh raised into goose bumps. He sensed that someone had just stepped closer to him—so close that he could feel them looming over his shoulder. But when he looked behind him, no one was there.

The guide nodded at the boy and his mother. "Cold spots are common throughout the jail. People also report voices calling for help or an uneasy feeling, as if someone is standing behind them, or even a feeling of being pushed from behind. If you take pictures, you might capture some orbs. We see a lot of those."

The boy took his mom's hand and pulled her out of the cell. He wasn't about to stick around to be pushed by whatever he felt behind him. As they walked away from Cell 17, the boy looked up and saw a noose in the gallows, swinging on its own. He tapped his mother's shoulder and pointed up.

The guide smiled at the boy and said, "That happens a lot too. It seems like the ghosts come and go. We think they're here to share their stories. They want to be remembered."

Pennhurst State School and Hospital
Spring City

Created as a home for people with mental illness and developmental and physical disabilities, Pennhurst State School and Hospital was originally called Eastern Pennsylvania State Institution for the Feeble-Minded and Epileptic. Construction began in 1903, and Pennhurst welcomed its first patient, listed in records simply as "Patient Number 1," on November 23, 1908.

In a time when people living with mental illnesses were considered unfit to coexist with the greater public, the state of Pennsylvania created Pennhurst as a solution to society's question of what to do with these tragically misunderstood people. Forced segregation seemed to be the answer. Administrators intended for Pennhurst to provide a safe environment for them to live out their lives in peace, separated from the rest of society.

Of course, it's easy to look back at the flawed logic, but at the time, the greatest medical minds proclaimed it to be the best course of action for everyone involved. Believing that they were doing the right thing, countless people placed their loved ones into institutions. Unsure of how to care for them on their own and without community support in place, many parents sent their children to Pennhurst as a last resort.

On the outside, Pennhurst was beautiful. Comprised of various brick structures with manicured lawns, it was a city within itself. It had its own farm, greenhouse, barbershop, and medical staff. But what began as a vision of tranquility and care soon blurred into a place of heartache and agony.

Four years after it opened, Pennhurst surpassed its maximum capacity. The facility was pressured into admitting individuals deemed undesirable who were not suffering from mental health issues—such as orphans, immigrants, and criminals. Concerned parties raised questions as early as 1912 about the fairness of placing patients with mental illness alongside those with epilepsy.

In 1913, the Commission for the Care of the Feeble-Minded officially declared individuals with mental illnesses to be "unfit for citizenship." They were considered a "menace to the peace" of society, and the commission believed the answer to resolving the risk they posed was to "break the endless productive chain." The commission's words were haunting in their own right. The goal was not treatment. It was isolation and, eventually, elimination.

Pennhurst essentially became a container for this goal. While many of its doctors and staff had the best intentions—to keep residents safe, protecting them from themselves and from one another—they lacked the resources to do so effectively. Experience was not required to work there, and training was minimal. The facility was understaffed, and the employees struggled to care for the volume of patients with such profound needs. For example, wards might only have two staff members for 60 or more individuals.

Higher-functioning residents helped care for those with more severe disabilities, and anyone who was able to work in other areas did. Some worked the farms, while others cleaned. Some even prepared and transported dead bodies to the morgue. Many residents worked full-time jobs, but no one ever paid them.

Residents with physical disabilities spent their days and nights in large cribs, with very little interaction and virtually no stimulation. Some patients were drugged to keep them docile, even if they didn't medically need it.

One resident recalled the fear everyone felt when night came and the lights went out. In the darkness, residents, deprived of normal human intimacy, would prowl and attack, taking what they felt they needed. Sexually transmitted diseases were common.

Years after the facility closed, one aide admitted that many babies were born at Pennhurst. Some were put up for adoption, some became residents themselves, and others were "disposed of" in incinerators—an accusation so appalling that the aide reportedly choked on the words as she said them.

Bill Baldini was a young reporter in 1968 when he got a tip about the local institution and its terrible conditions. What he documented with his camera crew was beyond any nightmare he could have dreamed.

"My crew was mortified," Baldini later said. "I had trouble keeping them on the job because they were literally getting sick from what they saw."

The conditions were so disturbing that it would be forever etched in their minds. Children, from infants to 5-year-olds, were lying in metal cages. They were covered in their own feces and were unable to walk because their muscles had atrophied from lack of use. Older children were tied to their beds. Skeletally nude men swayed to music inside their minds or were curled into balls, their pinched faces expressionless and hollow.

The sounds of the place were haunting, a deafening symphony of moans and cries. The smells were nearly unbearable. The stench of human excrement was so strong that it burned the crew's nostrils and made their eyes water.

By the time Pennhurst closed its doors to the public, it had admitted more than 10,000 patients. It's estimated that about half of those died there. There's no doubt that the residents suffered in conditions that most of us cannot fathom. In one study, nearly every survivor who was able to speak reported suffering abuse while living in the institution. Most arrived as children. Growing up within its walls forever imprinted their lives with the chaos and misery they witnessed and endured. Abuse was perpetrated by other patients, as well as by some of the staff. In 1983, nine aides were indicted on charges of beating and abusing patients, including some victims who were in wheelchairs. The many horrors were a catalyst for change that would ultimately protect the dignity and well-being of people with disabilities.

Legal battles waged against Pennhurst in the 1970s and early 1980s helped ensure rights to education and other protections for people with disabilities. Between March 17, 1978, and December 9, 1987, all residents of Pennhurst were relocated to small group homes in neighborhoods across southeastern Pennsylvania.

Today, visitors are able to take historical tours of the property, and the administrative building was converted into a haunted attraction. While that might sound tacky, the owners have made great efforts to honor the victims who once lived in the institution. To respect people with disabilities, the owners gave creative control of the attraction to a group of performers with disabilities, some of whom have been in institutions themselves. The site also hosts a paranormal convention each year, where attendees can meet some of their favorite ghost-hunting personalities.

Housed next door to the haunted attraction is the Pennhurst Memorial and Preservation Alliance. This organization is devoted to educating others about the wrongs that occurred at Pennhurst. In remembering the past, we can all help to make sure we learn from it and never allow it to be repeated.

* * *

Two security guards, hired by the property owner, stood outside Mayflower Hall. Having worked this shift many times before, keeping trespassers away, both men were familiar with the grounds. They'd already spent hours walking outside the collection of buildings that Pennhurst had grown into over the years. With the entire community connected by a labyrinth of underground tunnels, the guards had their work cut out for them if they were to keep the property—above- and belowground—secured.

Since Pennhurst's closure in 1986, reports of paranormal activity had come from various locations across the campus. Many ghostly encounters occurred within Mayflower Hall, Quaker Hall, Devin Hall, and the tunnels. With a history so entrenched in darkness, Pennhurst became a magnet for curious amateur ghost hunters looking for a thrill. These impromptu paranormal investigations were not only unwelcome, but their presence was also unsafe.

This evening, the two guards received a report of activity inside the Mayflower building. They steadied themselves as they stood outside the front door, preparing to enter. It was hard to guess what they might find.

Both men were familiar with eyewitness accounts of paranormal activity. Several of their colleagues had reported events ranging from sounds of crying and screaming to the appearance of shadow figures and doors slamming on their own. The harmonies of a phantom piano had been heard, and so had footsteps that seemed to scrape across the hallway floors.

Mayflower and Quaker Hall, former resident halls where volatile patients lived, were two of the grounds' paranormal hotspots. Security staff were often called to investigate reports of intruders in the buildings, only to find them completely empty. Visitors and staff sometimes reported being pushed or even having things thrown at them by mysterious forces.

The guards had also heard stories about Devin Hall, a dormitory where children were housed. There were sounds of slamming doors and whispers—and one witness, as they walked past a bathroom, heard a disembodied voice say, "They had no teeth." While that seemed random, Pennhurst had dentists on staff who removed residents' teeth.

The guards were relieved that they hadn't been called to investigate an intruder in the tunnels. The underground labyrinth, connecting more than 1 million square feet of buildings and over 100 acres of land, was considered the creepiest paranormal hotspot of all. Along with reports of slamming doors and disembodied voices, even more startling was the sheer number of apparitions reportedly seen beneath the surface of the campus. They included a woman in a white dress, a young girl with blonde hair, and the half-torso of a man.

With so much reported paranormal activity, the guards could only hope to find a living person inside Mayflower. Teenagers seeking a thrill would actually be welcome sights.

They entered the dark building and cautiously moved from one room to another. Their footsteps grated across dirt and debris left by crumbling plaster and years of neglect. The men watched and listened for any sign of an intruder.

"Nothing," one guard said to the other.

"Yeah, it seems empty," the other agreed.

As they headed toward the front of the building, there was a shift in the air. It somehow became colder and heavier.

A voice seemed to whisper directly into their ears, "Get out."

The men hurried toward the door and rushed to make it outside.

"Did you hear that?" one asked, his eyes wide.

"It was like someone was beside me, talking right into my ear," the other replied. "And it felt like someone was pushing me toward the door."

"I felt the same thing."

The two men stood in the moonlight, looking back at the brick structure, shaken by what they had just experienced.

It seems that, from the moment of Pennhurst's conception, it was doomed to be haunted, plagued by the horror of humankind's failed attempts to control that which we do not understand. The sadness and fear of thousands of souls have seeped into the concrete and plaster. Each haunting voice and every apparition are reminders of a time when our nation failed to protect its citizens. Echoes of their souls still cry out in the darkness for help that never came.

Dixmont
State Hospital
Pittsburgh

S ometimes, the best intentions fall short. The
Dixmont State Hospital is proof that mental-
health reform has been needed for centuries. Yet,
even when a facility has the most modern advancements
and is founded on cutting-edge principles, it can only
be as good as the science that supports it. And when a
facility operates for decades in a way that causes pain
and suffering to those it is supposed to help, it may just
end up haunted.

* * *

Dorothea Dix was born in Maine in 1802. After
traveling to Europe to seek alternative healthcare for
recurring illnesses, she became a passionate advocate
for mental healthcare reform. Up until the mid-1800s,
society's treatment of mental illness was punitive and
all-inclusive, meaning anyone could be institutionalized
for a number of reasons, ranging from alcoholism to

homosexuality. A person could even be sent away for being shy or disobedient.

The Department of the Insane in the Western Pennsylvania Hospital of Pittsburgh opened in 1862. By 1900, the facility cared for more than 1,500 patients. As a private hospital, the facility struggled with funding, especially during the Great Depression. The facility faced overcrowding. At times, beds even lined the hallways in the attic. Some stories suggest that unruly patients were sometimes chained to walls in the network of tunnels below the buildings. By 1946, the state took over the facility and renamed it the Dixmont State Hospital in honor of Dorothea Dix.

In the 1950s, as the treatment for mental illness evolved into lobotomy surgeries and electroshock therapies, a new building was specifically dedicated to these procedures. Further reform in the 1960s moved toward deinstitutionalization with the use of antipsychotic medications and with President John F. Kennedy's Community Mental Health Act. He was inspired by his sister Rosemary's botched lobotomy, and efforts were made to transition people with mental illness back into society.

Despite costly additions in the 1970s and a building at the site being added to the National Historic Register, the facility was closed in 1984. As the property sat vacant over the next decade, flooding, an arsonist's fire, and looting destroyed what was left of its value. Demolition began in 2006. Plans to build a Walmart on the site quite literally fell through when a landslide made the area too difficult to develop.

All that remains of the once-prominent treatment center is its cemetery with more than 1,300 graves, mostly for bodies of those who were forgotten by their families in death, just as they had been in life.

* * *

It was the graveyard that drew the high school girls to the former grounds of Dixmont State Hospital—that and their research paper that was due next week. They'd driven on Route 65, through the area where a landslide had covered a portion of the highway.

They parked near the skeleton of the old sign. Once clearly marking the cemetery, it was now just a weathered wooden frame. Behind it, a cement marker that read "Dixmont State Hospital Cemetery, Est. 1863" reassured them that they were in the right place.

"Can you believe that there used to be over a thousand people with mental illnesses living here in one place?" Leah asked.

"That's so sad," Jamie said quietly. "That's a lot of people who just got abandoned by their families."

The two walked slowly up the dirt road toward the heart of the cemetery. When they reached the plateau of the small rise, they paused and took in the scene before them. Hundreds of simple stone pillars, just 2 feet tall, peeked above layers of fallen leaves and underbrush.

The leaves crunched beneath their feet as they moved solemnly among the tree trunks, above forgotten souls buried in wooden boxes beneath their feet.

"Let's sit here," Leah said, settling near a broken marker. She opened her backpack and pulled out her notebook. She jotted a few notes, then said, "Here's what I have so far." She cleared her throat and began to read.

Despite its original good intentions, Dixmont State Hospital often failed to provide humane and helpful treatment. When a building's history includes stories of patients chained underground, traumatic electroshock therapy, and the likelihood of botched lobotomies, hauntings can almost be assumed.

After sitting abandoned for more than a decade, there has been plenty of time for ghost stories to emerge. Urban explorers and ghost hunters couldn't resist a chance to investigate an abandoned asylum, despite the very real dangers of asbestos exposure and dilapidated floors.

The most notable specter to make itself known was a tall, dark shadow figure that was said to guard the entrance to the morgue.

Stories from various paranormal investigations suggest that the shadow figure may have been a worker who was tasked with keeping patients out of the morgue. Others think that perhaps he was a patient himself, whose friend was sent to the morgue.

Investigators in this space have reported feeling cold blasts of air near the doorway. Apparitions were frequently seen wandering the grounds. When demolition workers were on the property, they often reported seeing faces peering at them from the windows. Any time this happened, demolition crews would be required to stop work to ensure that a human life wasn't at risk. Legends even state that the ghosts were so upset about the demolition, they were responsible for the landslide as an attempt to prevent further development of their forever home.

At one point during a paranormal investigation in the tunnels, an investigator asked if patients were tortured here. A disembodied voice immediately answered, "So much pain."

In the face of the trauma to living souls that comes with antiquated, harmful treatments, old institutions like the Dixmont State Hospital are destined to have chaotic energy. It's no wonder those souls might stay on to haunt the premises.

Leah set the notebook on her lap and looked around the graveyard.

"Do you think the cemetery is haunted too?" Jamie asked.

"I don't know," Leah replied. "But it feels cold, and I've got the heebie-jeebies just thinking about all of those tortured souls."

As if on cue, an overgrown nearby bush rustled, and a bird flew out.

The girls jumped.

Jamie stood up. "I'd rather not find out."

They snapped a quick photograph together, proof that they did site research for their project—the main reason for their visit. Then, the two walked away from the cemetery a little faster than when they had approached it. After all, the buildings in which the souls once roamed were no longer there. Those souls might have moved to the only remaining piece of the place they called home, forever standing guard over the bodies of those who never got to leave.

Harrisburg
State Hospital
Harrisburg

Albert Einstein once said, "Energy cannot be created or destroyed; it can only be changed from one form to another." So, when a building houses more than 150 years of chaotic, unstable energy, that energy doesn't just disappear.

* * *

Built in 1851, Harrisburg State Hospital, initially called the Pennsylvania State Lunatic Hospital, was the state's first facility designed to treat mental illness. The hospital was initially a single building with a large center structure that was four stories high and topped with a dome. This is where the superintendent, his family, and various other staff members lived. By 1852, three sets of wings jutted off the center structure where residents were housed. Female patients lived in the right wings, while the male patients lived in the left. The more violent and noisy residents lived in the farthermost parts of the wings.

Records show that the first patient to enter the hospital was 42-year-old Elizabeth B. from Londonberry Township. Elizabeth had recently lost two of her three children to scarlet fever and was said to suffer from "dyspepsia," otherwise known as an upset stomach, and "melancholy," both of which seemed logical, given her circumstances.

By 1867, the hospital was overcrowded. By 1893, the main building was in such a state of disrepair that the facility was torn down and replaced by a series of smaller structures across the campus. At its largest by 1912, the hospital included more than 70 buildings and over 1,000 acres of land, including farmland where patients were assigned to "work therapy." This involved growing food and raising livestock, which allowed the hospital to be self-sufficient. Full capacity was officially 2,019 patients, but at one time, the hospital held 2,441.

Legend has it that the old graveyard was moved during this time to make room for Hemlock Hall. An article in the local newspaper called for people to contact the acting superintendent and claim the bodies of their loved ones. However, many of the bodies went unclaimed, and there is no record of what became of them. Some believe that the bodies were simply buried elsewhere on the property.

Could bodies remain there, in unmarked graves, throughout the campus grounds? Given the period of time, it's a reasonable conclusion. There weren't any laws that governed where bodies could be buried.

Simple and affordable solutions to relocate them were a likely recourse.

The facility took great care to provide patients with a high quality of life. They had weekly dances, movies, and access to a fully stocked library. Patients could be part of the hospital's band or orchestra alongside staff members. With a general store, an arboretum, and its own power plant, the hospital became known as the "City on the Hill."

Unfortunately, in 1934, new superintendent Dr. Howard Perry introduced the latest treatments to the hospital. They included electroshock therapy and lobotomies. While the goal was to bring wellness to those who were suffering, the procedures only brought more suffering—and while Dr. Perry wasn't necessarily trying to torture his patients, that is exactly what was happening.

In 1971, new laws stated that patients could no longer be required to work or help the hospital operate. This took a heavy financial toll on hospitals that were essentially maintained by those who lived in them. Resident numbers declined steadily through the next three decades as better medications became available, and standards began to push for patients to return to their families or smaller settings in group homes.

On January 27, 2006, the hospital closed. Currently, the campus sits on 195 acres of land and consists of 50 buildings. Over the years, various state and private organizations have used the buildings for storage and office space, including an organization that used Hemlock Hall to house families with children experiencing homelessness.

In 2019, there was talk of selling the grounds and tearing down the buildings, but for now, Harrisburg State Hospital remains in the state's hands—with plans to create laboratory facilities for five state agencies.

* * *

The young boy tossed the ball against the wall, giggling as it bounced.

Long before the space had been turned into a gymnasium, it had simply been the basement of Hemlock Hall, a dormitory for patients at Harrisburg State Hospital. Now, families with nowhere else to go lived there while they got back on their feet. The basement was reimagined as a place for children to play.

"Did you see that one?" the boy asked as he scurried to catch the ball in his outstretched arms.

The nearby man smiled and nodded.

"That was my best catch yet!" exclaimed the boy.

The boy's sister and her friend ran down the stairs into the large, open space.

"Who are you talking to?" his sister asked.

"Mr. Apples," the boy replied, nodding toward the middle-aged man who wore a long, white lab coat.

"Oh, hi, Mr. Apples," replied his sister.

The girls grabbed jump ropes from a nearby bin and began twirling, hopping, and laughing.

The children had become accustomed to the kindly man who sometimes visited them in the basement. He seemed content to watch them play. His presence gave the children a sense of calm that they couldn't explain. They weren't sure where he came from or why he wore a lab coat, but they knew he was kind and meant them no harm.

"Watch this, Mr. Apples," the boy's sister called. She twirled the rope with her hands crossed in front of her and swiftly jumped through the opening.

The man clapped, delighted by her skillful display.

The children played for nearly an hour before their mother came down to get them. As they hurried toward the doorway, the boy turned and waved goodbye to the kind man who stood back in the shadows.

"Who are you waving at?" his mother asked, although she already knew the answer.

"Mr. Apples," the boy replied.

His mother squinted toward the darkened corner, knowing she wouldn't see anyone but wishing maybe she would.

The gym was empty—no surprise. The kids often talked about playing with the mysterious man, but no adult had ever seen him, despite thorough searches of the area. There was speculation among the adults that perhaps it was the ghost of a doctor who was murdered in 1930 by Moses Sweet.

Sweet was a patient at Harrisburg at the time, and he was angry about not being allowed to see his wife. Witnesses said he spoke to Dr. Miller for a moment during the doctor's rounds on the morning of January 8. When Miller turned to speak with another patient, Sweet attacked, slitting Miller's throat with a razor blade that had been smuggled into the hospital by a friend. The newspaper reported that it took the poor doctor 15 minutes to bleed out.

The kids' mother shivered at the thought. It seemed like such a terrible way for someone to die—especially someone devoted to caring for others. She looked down at her son. His smile beamed back at her. Clearly, the man's presence pleased the children.

She smiled and waved toward the empty gym. "Goodbye, Mr. Apples. Thank you for looking after the children."

* * *

With countless "insane" criminals living within its walls, with a number of documented murders and suicides that occurred on campus, and with a population of patients tormented by their own minds, it's no surprise that some of their residual energy might remain. Former staff and patients reported ghostly encounters even before the hospital closed its doors.

One paramedic recounted seeing a strange shadow figure after he was called to the hospital to aid an older gentleman with heart troubles. When he arrived, the man was talking to people in the room whom no one else could see. The responder recalled how hot it was that day, yet there was a strange chill in the air as he and his team worked on the patient. The paramedic soon realized that there might be more to this man's ravings than met the eye. He noticed a strange, shadowy figure in the corner of the room that seemed to watch them as they worked.

Years later, employees of businesses that utilized the former hospital as office space experienced phenomena they could not explain. From heavy footsteps stomping down empty hallways to apparitions of patients on gurneys being wheeled out of elevators, the reports are chilling.

If energy cannot be destroyed, as Albert Einstein suggests, what becomes of human energy after death?

At Harrisburg State Hospital, it seems to come out in the form of good old-fashioned hauntings. Although the walls of these structures could one day be knocked down, for now, at least, that energy remains.

Hill View Manor
New Castle

In days past, there weren't always good options for taking care of those who couldn't take care of themselves. When survival was a day-to-day concern, every family member had to contribute—and those who couldn't were considered a liability.

In the late 1800s, institutions were formed across the country as a necessity for taking care of the nation's rejected and destitute. These homes became receptacles for lost souls, and it makes sense that so much desperate energy would linger on after the building's original purpose had been served.

* * *

Originally called the Lawrence County Home, Hill View Manor opened in October of 1926. As a designated poor farm, its purpose was to provide a home for the poor, those with mental illnesses, and any others who were labeled by society as outcasts. Records of similar institutions indicate that their residents often included unwed mothers and orphans.

In 1944, original superintendents Mary and Perry Snyder were in their 70s. Suspected of mismanagement and negligence, they were asked to resign. By then, federal aid and assistance were already beginning to evolve to support families more efficiently. Those who were destitute no longer needed to be sent to poor farms. The mission of the Lawrence County Home shifted to serve a different community need: housing the elderly.

The facility remained in operation until 2004, when it was closed for financial reasons. By that time, Hill View Manor had everything it needed to serve its residents on-site, including laundry machines, recreation rooms, a hair salon, and even a morgue.

In the years since, the manor has changed hands many times. Now, the building hosts historic and haunted tours. While almost everything has been cleared out, some of the original fixtures, furnishings, and even personal belongings of the building's former residents remain, providing today's tourists with an eerie glimpse of what life as a resident must have been like in the institution.

In nearly 100 years of operation, thousands called Hill View Manor home—and hundreds died within its walls. Suicide was not uncommon. Several bodies were found hanging inside the building, while others chose to throw themselves out of windows on the upper floors. Many of those who died at Hill View Manor are buried on the grounds, often in unmarked graves.

* * *

"Good morning, Miss Beth," the nurse said cheerfully as she walked into the room. Her rubber-soled shoes squeaked as she moved across the linoleum toward the window.

"Good morning," Beth replied from a small chair in the corner of the room, where she sat knitting. Her voice was surprisingly strong for a woman of her age. She was nearing her 100th birthday in a few weeks and still did most tasks without assistance.

The nurse opened the window an inch to let in some fresh air. "It's wonderful outside today," she said. "We might have to get you ladies out for some sunshine before lunch." She turned and walked toward the bed across the room. "Good morning, Miss Gladys."

"She's still sleeping," Beth said nervously.

Beth's 95-year-old roommate was curled up under her covers. The tips of her white curls were barely visible above the edge of her blanket.

"You know she saw Jeffrey a few days ago," Beth said, her voice almost a whisper.

The nurse stopped walking and looked from Beth to Gladys. A pit formed in her stomach. She was well aware of the infamous ghost that the residents called Jeffrey.

Jeffrey, reportedly around 6 or 7 years old, was often seen wandering through the old nursing home. He was believed to be the spirit of a boy who had lived in the building when it was a poor farm. Supposedly, if a resident saw Jeffrey, their own demise would soon follow.

The nurse took a deep breath and continued toward Gladys's bed. She hesitantly pulled back the covers and felt the woman's cheek. It was cold to the touch. The mini-harbinger of death had struck again.

* * *

The countless paranormal events and numerous pieces of evidence gathered over the years at Hill View Manor are almost too great in number to classify. In addition to Jeffrey, other commonly reported occurrences include inexplicable cold spots, shadow figures, and orbs. Piano music is sometimes heard, floating through the walls with no discernable source. One visitor reported seeing a woman in a 1950s-style nurse uniform, walking the halls.

It is not uncommon for equipment and cell phone batteries to drain at unusually fast rates. Disembodied whispers float through the halls. Doors slam from abandoned and vacant rooms. Footsteps echo through the corridors.

It is estimated that at least 20 ghosts haunt Hill View Manor. Given that so many lost and forgotten souls were banished to this facility throughout its decades of operation, how could one possibly get an accurate count?

Betsy Ross House
Philadelphia

Born on New Year's Day in 1752, Elizabeth "Betsy" Griscom was the eighth of 17 children and one of only nine to survive childhood. After attending a traditional Quaker school, Betsy studied as an apprentice to an upholsterer, and she became a skilled seamstress. She fell in love with another upholstery apprentice, John Ross. However, Betsy's family did not approve. As a Quaker, Betsy was not allowed to marry outside her faith.

On November 4, 1773, at age 21, Betsy eloped with John and was cast out of her family. The penalties imposed by the Quaker religion required that she be cut off both financially and emotionally.

Betsy adopted her new husband's religion and attended services at Christ Church, sometimes sitting next to George Washington, who had been named America's commander in chief.

Betsy and John started their own upholstery business. On the cusp of the Revolutionary War, they made uniforms, tents, and flags.

In January of 1776, as a member of the Pennsylvania militia, John was fatally wounded during an explosion. Just three years after they had eloped, Betsy's beloved husband was dead, leaving her a widow at age 24.

During the summer of 1776, it is said that George Washington, Robert Morris, and John's half-brother George visited Betsy to recruit her for an important task. They showed her a sketch of a flag with 13 red-and-white stripes and 13 six-pointed stars. Legend has it that Betsy instead suggested five-pointed stars because they were easier to sew. After that fateful meeting, she reportedly sewed together the first United States flag.

Betsy remarried in June of 1777 and had two daughters. Unfortunately, one died as a child. In 1782, her second husband died of a fatal illness.

She married again in May of 1783. Together, they had five daughters, four of whom survived. In 1817, at the age of 65, Betsy lost her third husband to illness.

When she retired from her work as an upholsterer and seamstress, she went to live with one of her daughters. She loved to tell stories to her grandchildren. Betsy died in 1836, shortly after turning 84.

Her grandson, William Canby, submitted a paper to the Historical Society of Pennsylvania in 1870. In it, he shared the stories that his grandmother had recounted about how she was commissioned to make the flag for the Continental Army. While his claims lacked official documentation, he rallied his relatives to share their own accounts of his grandmother's story.

Despite a lack of tangible evidence that Betsy Ross created the first American flag, she is undoubtedly a symbol of American patriotism. Her life represents the survival and grit needed by the earliest Americans. A successful businesswoman, disowned by her family, she epitomized the American dream of freedom to choose her own religion and freedom to provide for her family, regardless of her gender.

The historic Betsy Ross House in Philadelphia is a tribute to her life and her work. In 1975, in conjunction with the Bicentennial, Betsy's grave was moved from Mount Moriah Cemetery—with permission from her descendants—to the courtyard of the Betsy Ross House.

* * *

It had been a long day, and the museum director was anxious to finish some paperwork before she headed home for the evening. She settled into the desk in her office, in the attic of the historic home. After a busy afternoon with many curious visitors, it felt good to be off her feet. She let herself sink into the chair to just breathe for a moment.

She listened to the silence, broken only by an occasional creak as the old home sheltered her from the wind outside. The house had been through hundreds of years of renovations and restorations, surviving a multitude of purposes. Yet the bones of the home remained strong—they just creaked every now and then, as old bones tend to do.

She let out a long breath, then leaned over the desk, determined to get through her work. It wasn't long before the energy of the room seemed to shift. Suddenly, the peace she'd felt was replaced by an unsettling realization that she was no longer alone.

She couldn't put her finger on how she knew that. She just knew. Her mind raced as her heartbeat quickened. She was well aware of the house's haunted reputation, and she knew that, even as recently as 1980, a man had been murdered in the basement: Two security guards had an altercation, and one shot the other three times before leaving him overnight to die alone. Museum visitors over the years reported hearing disembodied voices coming from the crime scene. Paranormal investigators even captured an EVP (recorded voices not heard by those present) of a man moaning in that area.

She knew the ghost story of a woman dressed in colonial-era clothing, crying in the basement, and had heard visitors and staff alike talk about phantom voices floating through the halls. People even believed in the presence of a polite ghost because there'd been reports of a disembodied voice saying, "Pardon me."

What she sensed in that moment didn't feel very polite. It felt menacing. She wondered if the dark presence—occasionally felt in the home's parlor—had followed her into the office. Or maybe it was a previous owner who had passed away when this space was their bedroom.

She tried to shake the thoughts from her mind and return to work. But before she could get started, a large, strong, unseen hand grabbed her shoulder. She screamed and jumped from the chair.

When she surveyed the office, no one else was there. Still, she felt trapped. The idea of moving across the room and through the house on her way to the front door terrified her. At the same time, the idea of being in the house a minute longer was more than she could bear. She looked toward the window; from outside, an American flag gently flapped against it. Afraid of whatever had grabbed her, she rushed to the window, threw it open, and climbed onto the flagpole.

It's unlikely that she saw humor in her situation. Escaping from a ghost in the home where the first American flag was made, she was crawling from a window onto a flagpole holding an American flag. But maybe the ghost responsible was able to appreciate the moment's poetic nature.

It's impossible to know for sure what the director experienced that evening. But with more than 250 years of history, the house that Betsy Ross once called home could be haunted. So many lives have been lived there, and countless moments of laughter and tears undoubtedly unfolded within its walls. The history of the location is enough to pique the interest of any ghost-story enthusiast. Add a brutal murder in the basement and a woman so frightened by a ghostly encounter that she escaped on a flagpole, and you have a recipe for intrigue.

Sayre Mansion
Bethlehem

R obert Heysham Sayre commanded respect. He was not only an important person in his community but was considered one of the most successful men in all of Pennsylvania. He rose in the ranks of the Lehigh Valley Railroad from apprentice to chief engineer and founded an iron-making company that operated for nearly 150 years. He was instrumental in the development of several landmarks in Bethlehem, including Lehigh University and the Episcopalian Cathedral Church of the Nativity, and he served as a trustee of St. Luke's Hospital. He was so revered that a community in Bradford County was named after him.

Sayre was a proud family man. In 1858, he built an opulent home for his growing family in the area that would become the heart of Bethlehem. He moved into the home on June 28, 1858, with his wife, Mary Evelyn, and their children.

Prior to the home's construction, two of their children passed away. But the young family would grow in the years ahead. All told, Mary Evelyn and Robert had nine children. But death would strike the Sayre family time and time again. By 1869, Robert had lost two more children and his wife, leaving him a widower with five surviving children.

Before his death in 1907, at the age of 82, Robert Sayre had buried three wives and five children. Seven of the family's deaths, including Mr. Sayre's, occurred within the walls of this gothic Victorian mansion. It's easy to assume that the home was shrouded in heartbreak, but despite those hardships, this was a place filled with laughter and love. It was a shelter from the storms of life, even when the storm brewed from within as the family grieved the loss of their own.

The Sayre Mansion has stood proudly on its perch in the Fountain Hill neighborhood for more than 165 years. For a time, it served as a fraternity house. Later, in the 1930s, it contained eight apartments. By 1990, there was talk of demolition due to decades of neglect and deterioration. Thankfully, a local couple saw the home's potential. The restoration cost the new owners millions of dollars. Returned to its original glory, it now serves guests as a bed-and-breakfast.

* * *

All the guests had been checked in, and Angela's work for the day was done. She would attend to the guests again in the morning. She settled into the bedroom on the first floor, which occupied the space that was once Robert Sayre's personal library.

It was a comfortable room, but for some reason, she struggled to fall asleep. Perhaps she was worried about getting everything ready for breakfast in the morning, or maybe it was just the general feeling of sleeping in a space that was not her own. Whatever the cause, Angela battled for sleep before finally drifting off. Her rest would be short-lived.

Angela's eyes snapped open, and she glanced at the clock: 1 a.m.

What woke me? she wondered.

Was it a sound she heard or something she'd felt? Her heart beat at a quickened pace, as if she'd been startled. But she couldn't figure out why or how.

And then she understood: She was not alone.

She glanced at the open space beside her. It was empty, yet she clearly felt the shifted weight of the mattress, as if someone was lying there. No matter how she tried to rationalize what was happening, she could not deny that, while the space next to her appeared empty, it was not.

Seconds seemed to stretch on endlessly as Angela felt frozen by fright and helplessness. She waited for hours, hoping for the fear to subside as she drifted in and out of a restless sleep—until any hope of sleep came crashing down . . . literally. The curtain rod hanging over the window was pulled out of the wall and clanked onto the floor.

Could Sayre's spirit have been frustrated to find a stranger sleeping in a bed where his desk used to be?

* * *

Since opening Sayre Mansion's doors to the public, staff and guests have reported numerous ghostly encounters. Accounts include hearing disembodied voices and footsteps, seeing shadow figures darting across hallways, and glimpsing a woman in a mirror gazing over guests' shoulders as they brush their hair. People have even felt their clothing being tugged by unseen hands.

With staff and guests frequently awakened in the dead of night by strange disturbances, something otherworldly must cohabitate with the living at the Sayre Mansion. Do the souls of the Sayre family remain, tangled in a loop of the lives they're no longer living? Or could the paranormal activity be connected to something darker?

An 18th-century map of the land could hold the answer. Long before the foundation was built for the beautiful mansion, something else was housed within the soil of the gently sloping plot of land: a cemetery.

As any horror buff can attest, building a house on a graveyard is a fast track to its haunting.

Gonder Mansion & Strasburg Cemetery
Strasburg

Strasburg is one of the most historic towns in the heart of Pennsylvania Dutch Country. While Strasburg has many beautiful homes within its city limits, one in particular stands out among the rest. Touted as "Strasburg's architectural crown jewel," the Gonder Mansion is located in the heart of town. With twin turrets and a classic Queen Anne style, the stately Victorian mansion was built by Benjamin B. "BB" Gonder, a local railroad tycoon.

He and his wife, Mary, had two children. During the home's construction, his family conveniently lived across the street in a modest house. From there, they monitored the construction process. Joining them in their home was BB's unwed sister, Annie.

Annie garnered a reputation in the community as being "simple-minded." According to stories, Mary, Annie's sister-in-law, was often embarrassed by Annie's behavior, especially when the family was entertaining male guests. Apparently, Annie would laugh too loudly at what male guests would say, especially if the men were attractive.

The mansion was completed in March of 1905. It was said to be the most beautiful house in town. But when it came time for the family to move in, Annie received quite a surprise. She was not invited to join the others in their home. Instead, she would remain in the small house across the street.

Annie's puzzling circumstances quickly became the talk of the town. Some speculated that she was ostracized after a fight with her brother or his wife. Some believed that her odd and awkward nature was to blame. Most had an opinion on whether or not Annie should have been allowed to remain under the same roof as her family.

There were reports that Annie couldn't comprehend her exile. In her loneliness, she was often seen staring out her window at the mansion in which she wasn't allowed to live. Some stories claim she looked so long and hard at the house that she talked about seeing faces in the stucco. She spoke of a face that frowned at her and another that smiled. It is said she believed the faces were mocking her. Annie swore revenge on Mary.

On March 16, 1916, BB suffered a heart attack and died in the Gonder Mansion. Annie's loneliness grew after her brother's death. On May 28, 1918, at the age of 61, she escaped from the care of her nurse. She boarded the 12:10 p.m. trolley, bound for Lampeter. She stayed at the Lampeter station until 1:20, when she boarded a return trolley to Strasburg.

She got off the trolley at its first stop, Edisonville Station, which was located halfway between Lampeter and her home in Strasburg. While exiting the trolley, she curiously asked the conductor, Willis Baldwin, if he knew how deep Pequea Creek was in Edisonville. This was the last time anyone saw Annie alive.

Her hat and purse were found floating in the waters of Pequea Creek. In the early morning hours of May 29, her body was found submerged there. Deputy coroner J. Ross Hildebrand ruled her death to be a suicide by drowning.

Annie's body was buried in Strasburg Cemetery. Since her brother and parents preceded her in death, it's likely that her gravesite would have been chosen by Mary. It sits off to the side, on the far left of the Gonder family plot. Her headstone is turned, and it faces away from the rest of her family. It seems that, even in her death, she has been shut out and shunned in disgrace.

Not long after Annie's death, reports of a haunting at the mansion began. Those in the home heard loud laughter from a woman when no women were present. Strangely enough, only men seemed able to hear it. Passersby also reported seeing her ghost sitting in one of the mansion's windows.

It seems that, in death, Annie took matters into her own hands and is enjoying a different view—this time from inside her brother's home.

The story of Annie's ostracism is haunting on its own. Everyone deserves to be loved, especially by their family. If the legends are true, to be shunned by society for laughing or finding too much excitement in others' company is a terrifying tragedy.

* * *

A cloud rolled over the crescent moon, darkening the landscape. The carload of teens slowed to a stop near the Gonder family plot.

"There it is," a boy said from the backseat.

"Alright, Emma, you have to touch it," a girl beside her said.

Emma shifted in the passenger seat and took a deep breath as she looked at the stone, angled strangely away from the other family markers. She shrugged, "No problem." Her voice sounded braver than she felt, but she never backed down from a dare.

All the local kids knew something—or someone—haunted Strasburg Cemetery. It wasn't unusual for a few teens to stop for a thrill late at night, hoping to glimpse one of the ghosts said to roam there. They watched for the spirit of a young boy and a little girl said to wander among the stones. Or, like Emma and her friends, they came to find the lost soul of Annie Gonder staring at her grave or strolling across the grounds.

Emma flung the passenger door open and jumped from the car. She moved quickly across the grass and placed her hand on the gravestone that read:

Annie K. Gonder
December 8, 1856
May 28, 1918

As she turned, prepared to race back to the car, she saw a strange mist rolling slowly around the nearby gravestones. Her heart jumped and her breath caught in her throat.

Was it her imagination, or was it moving toward her? She wasn't going to stick around to find out. She sprinted toward the open passenger door of the car. She could hear her friends inside, yelling, but couldn't make out what they were saying.

She leaped inside and slammed the door shut. Her friend threw the gear shift into drive and sped toward the black iron gate that marked the graveyard's entrance.

"Go, go, go!" the girl next to Emma screamed.

As the car bounced over the apron of concrete that separated the cemetery path from the street, Emma looked back toward Annie's grave. It was then that she saw what her friends had been screaming about. A strange white light and the eerie mist had settled at the very spot where Emma had been standing.

They weren't the first to witness this manifestation, and they wouldn't be the last.

Graeme Park
Horsham

In the study of history, some places seem to be containers for misery, while others are a respite for peace. Graeme Park, with its beautiful streams, ponds, and lush grassy knolls, is a place to remember the good times more than the sad ones. Perhaps some souls who once lived there continue to call this oasis home.

* * *

With 42 acres of land—complete with nature trails and a historic mansion built in 1722 by colonial Pennsylvania Governor Sir William Keith—Graeme Park is a popular tourist attraction and wedding venue.

Dr. Thomas Graeme purchased the property in 1739. He was married to Sir William Keith's stepdaughter, Ann. Graeme's only surviving child, Elizabeth, inherited the property in 1772, making her the third-generation family member to own the estate.

Before her father passed away, Elizabeth married a Scottish immigrant named Henry Hugh Fergusson. He embodied the definition of a "starving artist." He was a penniless poet who was deeply loyal to the crown. He abandoned his wife and returned to England.

Because of Fergusson's loyalty to Great Britain, the colonial government seized Elizabeth's property, claiming that it was owned by a traitor. Elizabeth found herself without her home or her husband, but she wasn't without hope.

Elizabeth was well-known for the literary salons she hosted. Many of society's political elite—including such prominent figures as American Founding Fathers Dr. Benjamin Rush, John Dickenson, and Francis Hopkinson—enjoyed attending the events and were deeply fond of Elizabeth. As she fought for her family estate, they came to her defense. Three years after losing her home, she was able to regain it.

Following Elizabeth's death in 1801, Samuel Penrose purchased the estate. In 1920, the Strawbridge family purchased the property and lived there for 38 years before donating 42 acres, including the mansion, to the Commonwealth of Pennsylvania.

Today, the home is a National Historic Landmark, enjoyed by many visitors. With original woodwork throughout and many of its original features, entering the Keith House is like stepping back in time. Visitors can take historic tours of the home—complete with re-enactors—or simply take in the beauty of the grounds.

* * *

Betsy Stedman had been one of Elizabeth Graeme's best friends. They were so close that Betsy had shared her own home and small inheritance with Elizabeth after the government confiscated the Graeme estate. The two were like sisters.

It was emotional for Betsy to be standing inside Elizabeth's beloved home on the heels of Elizabeth's death. Betsy was sad but also felt a sense of comfort in the place her friend loved most. Betsy spent a few moments in the parlor, recalling the lovely parties she'd enjoyed there. She wiped at a tear that slipped from her eye, and then she turned and walked toward the stairs that led to the bedrooms.

She was halfway up the steps when Elizabeth appeared on the stairwell, walking slowly downward. Betsy gasped. Her friend grew closer until they stood on the same step, their skirts brushing against one another. Elizabeth continued on.

After a few seconds of shock, Betsy turned to see if her friend was still there, but the stairwell was empty.

While it was startling to see Elizabeth's spirit after her passing, Betsy was hardly surprised. Where else would Elizabeth be? She treasured her home. Betsy had no doubt that, as long as the home stood, Elizabeth could be found there.

* * *

Over the years, witnesses have reported a variety of paranormal encounters, including seeing Governor Keith, hearing Elizabeth's skirts rustling on the main staircase, and hearing the closet door in the master bedroom locking and unlocking itself.

An account from a 1970s film crew involved a room in the house that had been a space of great happiness. The Graeme family was known for their grand parties and celebrations in the parlor. Elizabeth had many fond memories there. But when the Continental Army seized the property and sold all of her personal items at auction, the once-opulent parlor became an empty shell.

While filming scenes for a documentary in the parlor, the crew had an experience they could never quite explain. As the day ended, they set up for the next morning's shoot. They placed the hands of the grandfather clock at 3:00 because that was the time they would need the clock to read when they filmed. The doors and windows were closed and locked, and the alarm system was turned on. The next morning, the crew found the hands of the clock set to 12:00.

Puzzled, they reset the hands to 3:00 and commenced with their shoot. At the end of the day, they reset for the next day, once again making sure the hands were set to 3:00. Once again, the building was locked, and the alarm was set.

Again, when the staff returned the next morning, they found the hands of the clock had moved back to 12:00. Was the spirit of Elizabeth trying to let them know she was keeping an eye on them?

We can assume that Elizabeth's soul is delighted by the many visitors at Graeme Park. After all, she loved hosting get-togethers. She must be overjoyed to see families picnicking near the pond and couples getting married on the grounds. If wedding guests listen closely, they might even hear her satin skirt rustling as she joins the celebration.

King George II Inn
Bristol

An innate thrill comes from visiting a structure that dates back to the early settlers. Visitors can't help but imagine the lives that were lived within those walls during times so different from today. Each soul leaves behind impressions, like footprints that are swallowed by the sands of time—yet linger just beneath the surface. Sometimes, the veil is cracked open enough for the past to slip into the present, and a location becomes more than just historic; it becomes haunted.

* * *

Built along the banks of the Delaware River in 1681 by Englishman Samuel Clift, the King George II Inn is considered America's oldest continuously operating inn and tavern. It offered shelter, food, and drinks before the United States was even a nation. Clift built the public house—initially called the Ferry House—as a place for travelers who used his ferry service to cross the river. In 1765, the building was expanded to its present structure and renamed the King George II Inn.

With its proximity to such a vital waterway, the building served an important role in the Revolutionary War. In 1776, General John Cadwalader used the inn as his headquarters when his troop of nearly 3,000 soldiers was stationed in Bristol to guard the river. It's reported that General George Washington himself stayed there.

During the 1800s, the inn became a playground for the social elite. Men in top hats gathered around the shiny dark-wood bar top. Elegantly dressed women could often be found sipping tea in the sunlight that streamed through the picture windows, which overlooked the river. Over the years, the inn hosted such notable guests as President John Adams and President James Madison.

* * *

A long row of liquor bottles lined the bar top.

"It was a good night," one man said to the other. An owner of the King George II Inn, he was deeply invested in the success of the venue. Seeing all the bottles was confirmation that they were doing what they set out to do when he and his partner bought the historic location.

Thirty minutes earlier, the place had been packed. Music, laughter, and the sound of ice clinking in glasses were the anthem of a full house—and the empty liquor bottles were signs of a profitable evening.

The bartender walked down the line, counting those bottles—when two of the bottles shot across the bar and shattered against the wall. Both men looked in shock at the broken glass that had fallen to the floor.

"What just happened?" the owner asked. "I mean, I saw what just happened, but . . . how?"

The bartender shrugged. "Maybe the ghosts are upset that we didn't share."

* * *

With more than 340 years of history, the establishment has hosted a vast number of patrons and overnight guests. It wasn't uncommon for hotels to double as boarding houses, so it's likely that many people lived at the inn for extended periods of time.

How many wonderful occasions have been celebrated there? How many tears were shed behind closed doors? How many guests succumbed to death within these walls? These are questions that cannot be answered. However, over the years, the King George II Inn has garnered a reputation for being haunted.

One ghostly guest, in particular, has been reported on numerous occasions. Multiple witnesses have seen the apparition of a well-dressed man sporting a top hat. Some have even reported the apparition speaking to them. Others have seen him dancing, which is why he is often referred to as "the dancing ghost." Perhaps he's a wealthy patron from the inn's 19th-century days of social glory.

Patrons have reported feeling someone firmly press on their back when no one else is there. Staff say the sound of a baby crying has been heard in upper levels. Other paranormal activity includes doors slamming, pictures spontaneously falling off walls, and chairs being moved by unseen hands.

King George II Inn witnessed the birth of a nation. It has held the hopes and fears of more than three centuries. And it seems, from time to time, some energy slips through a crack from the past and dances for a moment in the present—just long enough to remind us of what once was.

Harmony Inn
Harmony

In 1856, wealthy industrialist Austin Pearce built a beautiful Italianate-style mansion at 230 Mercer Street, in the heart of Harmony. He was a prominent banker, railroad executive, and mill operator. With elaborate woodwork and indoor plumbing, Pearce's new home befittted his stature in the community.

When his railroad business failed, Pearce sold his magnificent home to the Ziegler family, descendants of Mennonite settlers.

The Ziegler family built a two-story addition and renovated the mansion into a hotel and saloon. Over the century that followed, the property changed ownership too many times to list. Each owner brought new visions, ideas, and changes.

In most of its time as a business, Harmony Inn has primarily been a two-story restaurant.

* * *

The couple settled down at the bar. Sally peered over her drink menu, surveying the room. Her husband, Scott, side-eyed her with a smile.

"What can I get you?" the bartender asked.

Sally looked at her menu, then went back to gazing at the dining room.

"I'll take an old-fashioned," Scott said. He looked at his wife and stifled a laugh. "Sally?"

"Oh, yeah . . ." Sally replied. "Um . . ."

"You're dying to ask about the ghost stories, aren't you?" Scott asked her.

The bartender smiled. "We get that a lot."

Sally smiled back. "Do you know the stories?"

The bartender nodded. "A lot of times, people feel like they're being watched. One of our owners was staying overnight, right here in the bar. He said he felt like someone was watching him all night. Music turns off and on by itself—lots of little things like that."

Scott and Sally both leaned forward.

The bartender added, "We've actually had security cameras pick up images of entities. One of the current owners saw an entity in the basement."

"That's cool," Scott said.

"I'll try the house martini," Sally said. "Have you seen anything personally?"

"Once, I was standing in the entryway of the whiskey cave and felt something touch my back. Then I saw some sort of strange shadow in there."

"Sounds scary," said Sally.

He shrugged. "It seems like the spirits are mostly mischievous. One of our other bartenders was doing inventory, and a mounted paper towel dispenser shot out about 40 paper towels in a row—that kind of thing. Not dangerous or scary, just trying to get our attention. I'll get your drinks," he said.

"I'm going to find the bathroom," Scott said, pushing himself away from the bar. "I'll be right back."

On the way back from the restroom, he passed the main staircase. Standing at the top of the landing on the second floor, looking down at him, was a young girl in a white dress. She seemed out of place, almost as if she'd stepped through the veil from a different time. He smiled and nodded at her. It was as if she was looking right through him . . . then she disappeared.

Scott hurried back to his seat as the bartender set his drink on a white napkin.

"If I told you I just saw a little girl in a white dress vanish before my eyes, would you think I was crazy?" Scott asked.

"You saw her on the stairs?" the bartender asked with a sly smile.

Scott nodded.

"We call her Emily," the bartender replied. "She's one of the ghosts upstairs."

"One of the ghosts?" Sally asked.

"People believe there's an older woman called Granny who took care of children with tuberculosis. Many of them didn't make it. They say when Granny died, her body was buried in the wall."

Sally's mouth dropped open. "Why?"

"I suppose to prevent the disease from spreading." The bartender shrugged before turning his attention to another patron.

Sally looked at Scott, her eyes wide. "There might be a dead body in the wall?"

Scott lifted his drink and held it toward her. "Cheers," he said with a smile.

Sally clinked her glass against his and then took a sip and looked around the room, wondering what other ghosts might be lurking throughout this place.

Brinton Lodge and the Free Love Valley
Chester & Philadelphia Counties

It's easy to become entranced by stories of specters or disembodied souls trying to reach us from beyond the grave, asking not to be forgotten. After all, ghost stories are intended to leave readers on the edge of their seats. Occasionally, though, the real history can be more intriguing than the ghosts that follow.

* * *

The area around Brinton Lodge was largely settled by families with German heritage. So, in 1837, when religious zealot Theophilus Ransom Gates met Hannah Williamson (a woman of "questionable character") and settled near Coventry Township in Chester County, the locals got some interesting new neighbors.

Gates is credited with starting the Battle Axes of the Lord, a movement that allowed members to prioritize sexual satisfaction and disregard the sanctity of marriage. Sect members were not only encouraged to choose other partners, but they were also told to change partners as many times as necessary to find the person with whom they were most compatible. Thus, the area ultimately became known as "Free Love Valley."

During gatherings, sect members were encouraged to remove their clothes—securing their status as an early nudist colony—and forget their morals.

A single woman of means, Hannah Shengel was a member of the Battle Axe cult. She regularly hosted orgies on her property—within the spring house that still stands today. Legend has it that she kept an axe under her bed as a means of protection. In 1855, she was brutally murdered in her bedroom with that very axe. The crime was never solved.

Before the grisly murder, the community was already beside itself with disdain for the sect, its teachings, and its loose morals. One local pastor was said to have had a nervous breakdown after preaching against the cult's teachings. In another local church, several Battle Axe members marched naked up the aisle during a service to promote their beliefs.

Ultimately, townspeople rallied. Law enforcement launched investigations, charging several members with violations of the marriage laws. Convictions for these violations humbled the cult's audacious behaviors.

When Gates died, Hannah Williamson became the cult's leader. But as the order lost momentum, she left Free Love Valley in 1857, setting out for the West as a missionary.

* * *

In the early 1900s, the Brinton Lodge property was purchased by the Wittman family. Having earned their wealth in iron, they expanded the simple farmhouse into an elaborate 28-room mansion, strangely built onto and around the original farmhouse.

During Prohibition, hotel owner Caleb Brinton purchased the mansion with a vision. He turned it into a gentlemen's club for the area's rich and famous. Guests included the likes of Elizabeth Taylor, Frank Sinatra, and Benny Goodman.

In 1972, a hurricane caused catastrophic water damage and flooding to the property. Without flood insurance, Brinton completely lost his investment. He died there on October 26, 1974.

The building was restored and turned into a restaurant in the 1980s. Today, the Brinton Lodge is owned by Hidden Brewing Company. The restaurant features craft beers and ciders produced on-site and a locally sourced dinner menu. The Lodge also offers historic ghost tours.

* * *

In the late 1970s, a medium who was known for his work as a psychic detective stayed at Brinton Lodge for several days. As he walked through the building with the caretaker of the property, he tuned in to the energy of the space.

"I can feel that there are five spirits here," he said to the caretaker. "I'm sensing Caleb Brinton. I can see him tipping his hat. He likes to tip his hat at the people who come through. His mother is here too."

"Yes," said the caretaker. "She lived here for many years after her husband died in 1944."

"Do people report paranormal phenomena in the lodge?" asked the psychic.

"Oh yes, people report seeing shadows sweep across the windows on the upper floors. Cold drafts are a common report by the staff and visitors without any reasonable explanation. And, every now and then, doors seem to lock by their own free will."

"Interesting," said the psychic.

"Visitors have seen a small girl."

"I feel like she might be Caleb's daughter," said the psychic, his eyes closed.

"There's also a ghost we like to call Dapper Dan."

The psychic added, "He's quite the ladies' man."

"Exactly," laughed the caretaker.

* * *

Famed psychic Lorraine Warren also visited the site of Hannah Shengel's murder. Without knowing anything of the area's strange cult and its history, she talked about the sexual rituals that used to take place there.

A nonresponsive ghost on the side of the road or the polite Mr. Brinton tipping his hat to visitors would be a sight to see, but the early cultish history of this location is as shocking as any haunted happening. A cult promoting promiscuity, nudity, and free love was able to thrive in a community that was known for its God-fearing people. And when one of its members was murdered with her own axe, it created a legend that will live on forever.

Hotel Bethlehem
Bethlehem

Will the afterlife be elegant? Perhaps a soul can choose to go where it experienced the finer things in life. If so, why wouldn't one want to revisit the most glorious luxury hotel of its time?

* * *

In 1741, members of a Protestant denomination called the Moravians began to settle 4,000 acres in what became the town of Bethlehem. Moravians lived in a self-sufficient, pacifist, religious community where everyone worked for the good of the whole and took care of each other.

The first structure on the property was built in 1741 and was called the First House of Bethlehem. This hotel offered refuge and lodging for leaders and patriots during the Revolutionary War. By 1823, a new hotel had been built on the site. Operating as the Golden Eagle Hotel, the establishment counted

Mark Twain and President Ulysses S. Grant among its distinguished guests.

In 1919, the hotel served as temporary housing for soldiers returning from the Great War. In 1921, steel tycoon Charles M. Schwab purchased the property and tore down the old hotel. He built a luxury hotel that featured state-of-the-art amenities and innovations, including fireproof steel beams, manufactured by his own company. The finished structure included a barbershop, a workout room, and luxury shops.

The hotel drew affluent guests from all over the country. Amelia Earhart attended a banquet in her honor at the hotel, arriving in her own plane. Winston Churchill, Henry Ford, and Thomas Edison were also hotel visitors. Multiple presidents have stayed in its rooms, including John F. Kennedy, Gerald Ford, and Bill Clinton. Stars like Shirley Temple and Muhammad Ali have also appreciated the hotel's famous hospitality. However, in January 1998, the hotel was forced into bankruptcy.

Fortunately, the Bethlehem Hotel was revived, renovated, and restored—saved by a franchising agreement. With new branding under the Radisson group's Historic Hotels of America, the Historic Hotel Bethlehem continues to offer guests the luxury on which it was founded.

* * *

The ghosts at the Historic Hotel Bethlehem have become almost as famous as some of the hotel's living patrons.

Francis Thomas was born in Germany in 1732. He emigrated to America with his family when he was 6 and became a follower of the Moravian faith. He had a reckless disregard for danger and was known to take excessive risks. At some point in his adulthood, he became the town guide of Bethlehem until his death in 1822. It is said that he still attends to the town's visitors by frequenting the Historic Hotel Bethlehem and is often seen around the hotel.

In 1833, the Golden Eagle Hotel was owned by the Moravian Church. Mr. and Mrs. Brong were landlords who oversaw the hotel. It soon came to the attention of the church that Mr. Brong liked to partake excessively of alcohol. The hotel bartender routinely had to find him a bench so he could lie down.

Mrs. Brong had an unusual habit: She was known to greet guests in the lobby barefoot. Mr. and Mrs. Brong were relieved of their duties after only six months. However, Mrs. Brong is still believed to visit with dinner guests and the hotel staff. They recognize her because she usually appears barefoot.

Mary Augusta Yohe was born in 1866 at the Golden Eagle Hotel. She was the granddaughter of Caleb Yohe, the hotel's proprietor at the time. She grew up singing at the hotel and entertaining the wealthy guests.

By 1888, Mary had become a star of the stage. She was also known in the gossip columns for her wild affairs. It is reported that Mary frequents the third-floor exercise rooms and the lobby of the hotel. Sometimes, the hotel's player piano mysteriously turns on. It is said that Mary's happiest times were spent entertaining hotel guests. Therefore, Mary gets the credit for playing the piano in her afterlife.

The hotel also has an infamous unknown guest. The apparition of a man is often seen in Room 932. He has appeared in reflections in the mirror. Papers have stood on end, and books have flown off the shelves. Photo evidence of orbs is frequently captured here.

Unlike some other haunted properties, the ghosts at the Historic Hotel Bethlehem seem refined and well-behaved—except, perhaps, Mrs. Brong, who could use some shoes. Then again, if she were wearing shoes, no one would know who she was.

Bube's Brewery
Mount Joy

lois Bube was born in the German state of Bavaria. He emigrated to America in 1869 at the age of 18. He found work in a brewery, and it wasn't long before he was running a small one of his own. Bavarian beer was all the rage in the United States, so Bube brewed it here, in addition to a pilsner-style beer, ale, and soda.

Bube was innovative in his methods and efficient with his operations. He used coal-fired steam to produce electricity to run his facility. The hotel even had the first flushable toilet in town. Thanks to the catacombs below the buildings, up to 700 barrels of beer could be stored year-round at a temperature of 50 degrees.

In 1908, at age 57, Bube died suddenly. Although his family tried to keep the brewery running, it was never quite the same. With the first World War raging, Bube's Brewery was unable to survive; it closed in 1917.

In 1920, Prohibition severely crippled all the nation's brewery businesses. Legend claims that Bube's operated as a speakeasy during Prohibition. The tunnels running below the brewery would certainly provide an element of safety for anyone breaking the dry laws.

Members of the family lived on-site until 1960. Restoration efforts began in 1968, and a museum opened there in 1970 to commemorate the brewery's 100th anniversary.

In 1982, at age 24, the brewery's current owner, Sam Allen, fell in love with the history of the brewery. Allen was passionate about honoring the history of the establishment while creating unique and entertaining dining experiences for patrons.

The brewery is always evolving with innovative, forward-thinking strategies. Allen strives, just like the brewery's original owner, Alois Bube, to keep it moving forward. He has added an escape room, interactive dinners with Victorian characters, and jazz nights. In a special homage to its history, the brewery also offers ghost tours.

* * *

Olivia and Maggie stood in the pub, waiting for their tour guide. They were the first to arrive and were 20 minutes early.

It wasn't long before several others arrived for the tour. A woman in one of the other groups spoke loudly about how people often felt uneasy in the pub. "The ghosts in here even blow out the oil lamps sometimes."

Olivia shivered. "Do you feel something?" she whispered to Maggie.

Maggie wrapped her arms around herself. "Yeah, and whatever it is, it's not good."

A woman carrying a clipboard came in from the back room. "Welcome to Bube's Brewery. My name is Mallory, and I'll be your tour guide. I'm excited to take you around this amazing historic property. Before I begin, how many of you have heard the ghost stories about this place?"

Olivia and Maggie raised their hands, along with several others.

"I encourage you to pay attention to everything as we walk through the building. A lot of paranormal activity can happen on these tours. Some folks have talked about seeing a man with a white beard. We believe that is the ghost of Alois Bube."

"Do you believe it's him?" asked a man.

"Given how passionate he was about his beloved brewery, I wouldn't be surprised if he stops in to check on us every now and then, even if it's just to see how things are going. I hope he's proud when he sees that something he started has survived this long and is being enjoyed by a new generation."

Everyone on the tour nodded.

"We've also had visitors report seeing the spirit of a young girl in a white dress, so keep an eye open for her too."

A woman raised her hand. "My friend saw her wandering in the art gallery. They asked what her name was, and she told them it was Amy."

"I heard about that tour," said their guide. "That would have been amazing to witness."

The woman nodded.

"When we go down into the catacombs, guests—usually women—report having their hair or hands touched. So pay attention when you're down there. One of our waitresses reported seeing a female figure with long hair who appeared and then disappeared."

"I can't wait to finally see what it looks like down there," whispered Maggie.

Olivia nodded.

"Let's get started with our tour," said their guide. "We're going upstairs first." She led the group out of the room and up the stairs.

After she was sure everyone was following, she said, "We're going into the ballroom." She led them into the space.

Olivia grabbed Maggie's arm and whispered, "They say that Alois Bube's granddaughter, Pauline, haunts this room."

"Pauline was the daughter of Henry Engle and Josie Bube," said the tour guide. "They managed and maintained the property from 1921 until 1960. It has been reported that Pauline suffered from schizophrenia. With minimal services available for mental illness, Pauline was kept isolated and spent a good deal of time in the family's residence."

"But it feels like something is in here now," Olivia said and shivered.

"Yeah," agreed Maggie, "but it feels better than it did downstairs. This feels happy. Whatever was downstairs felt darker."

* * *

Alois Bube has a lot to be proud of. His American dream was realized. Through hard work and innovation, he left a legacy that has lived on for more than 150 years. One can imagine his delight as he watches Sam Allen carry on that legacy with the same creativity and enthusiasm. It's almost as if Allen isn't working alone. Perhaps Bube is beside him, whispering in his ear as the two carry on that American dream together.

Mishler Theatre
Altoona

Many towns can credit their growth and development to railroad expansion in the mid-1800s. Altoona is no different. When the Pennsylvania Railroad expanded into the area, engineers were met with a challenge: how to construct a working rail line through the Allegheny Mountains. The solution was the infamous Horseshoe Curve, which became known as one of eight engineering marvels of the modern world.

Thanks to the railroad, in 1858, travel between Pittsburgh and Philadelphia could be accomplished in 15 hours instead of three days.

An 18-year-old man named Isaac Mishler arrived in Altoona in 1880, looking for work. He found it in a railroad repair shop. Several years later, he opened a cigar store on 11th Avenue. He also bought a local baseball team.

In 1893, Mishler took over the 11th Avenue Opera House. In 1905, Mishler put plans in motion to build and open a new theater. His vision came to life with the grand opening of the Mishler Theatre on February 15, 1906. This new theater promised a lavish entertainment experience. With 40 passenger trains stopping each day, Mishler had an endless supply of patrons.

Nine months later, a fire that began in a neighboring building swept through the theater. Despite state-of-the-art safety features, like a fireproof curtain and sprinklers, the interior of the building was destroyed.

Mishler immediately set out to rebuild. He salvaged the exterior walls, added a new roof, and installed even better fire safety features. The rebuilt theater opened just three months later.

In 1923, Mishler announced his retirement, and he sold the theater in 1931. Now managed by the Blair County Arts Foundation, the Mishler Theatre was named to the National Historic Register in 1973.

* * *

"What's that smell?" little Madeline Letsche asked, wrinkling her nose.

Her mother, Laura Letsche, smiled. She was in charge of setting up light and sound equipment for productions at the notoriously haunted Mishler Theatre. Visitors often reported smelling cigar smoke drifting through the air, and she could smell it now.

"That's probably just Mr. Mishler coming to check on guests," replied Laura. "When he was alive, he used to smoke. Some people say he comes back to visit and lets people know that it's him by his cigar smoke."

It wouldn't be the female ghost. She stayed in the ladies' restroom. Employees had reported seeing her there, dressed in 1930s clothing. The sinks in the restrooms had been known to spontaneously turn off and on.

"Is he a ghost?" asked Madeline.

"Yes," said Laura, "but not a scary one."

"Someone should tell him he's not allowed to smoke inside," said Madeline.

"Well, if you see him, feel free to say something," said her mother.

"Mama," asked Madeline, "can I go play?"

"Of course, but stay where I can see you," said her mother. "I'll be up there." She pointed to the upper balcony.

A short while later, Laura went to find Madeline. When Laura spotted her, Madeline appeared to be talking to someone—but no one else was there.

"It's time to go," Laura called.

She watched as Madeline waved goodbye.

"Who were you talking to?"

"Oh," said Madeline, "that was my friend."

"Was he smoking?" asked Laura with a smile. "Did you tell him he couldn't smoke inside?"

"Oh no," said Madeline seriously. "He never smokes around me. But I did tell him that if he saw anyone else smoking, he should ask them to stop."

Laura shifted uncomfortably. She hadn't really thought a ghost would show up to talk to her daughter. "Have you seen him here before?" asked Laura.

"Yes," said Madeline. "The first time, I was a little scared. I thought I was in trouble. He's very tall, but he is always nice to me. Today, he was wearing a big black hat. Last time, his hat was a floppy one. He likes to change into different hats for me."

"What do you talk about?"

"He tells me about the shows that used to be on the stage. I think he really loves his job here."

Laura relaxed. It was quite fascinating to think that her daughter's new friend was the founder of the theater himself—a man who had died 50 years before.

Fulton Theatre
Lancaster

Robert Fulton is one of Lancaster's most famous citizens. Born in 1765, he successfully commercialized the steamboat. In 1807, his steamboat, the *Clermont,* made its first successful run on the Hudson River, transporting 60 passengers.

Before the American Revolution, the site on which the Fulton Theatre sits was the location of a jail. On December 27, 1763, armed men known as the Paxtang Boys broke into the jail and murdered a group of Conestoga Indians being housed there for their safety.

In 1852, Fulton Hall was commissioned by Christopher Hager and designed by architect Samuel Sloan. The theater was built over the foundation of the old jail, utilizing the exterior wall of the original jail's courtyard as the back wall of the theater.

By 1910, movies stole customers away from live theater, and traveling shows were harder to find. By

1920, the Fulton added burlesque shows to its lineup, earning owner Charles Yecker an arrest for exhibiting immoral content. Over the next several years, the theater evolved into a movie house. In 1969, the Fulton was named a National Historic Landmark, making it one of only eight theaters in the country to be recognized as such.

Through the years, stars like Mark Twain, Lily Tomlin, Duke Ellington, and Louis Armstrong have graced its stage.

* * *

Over many years throughout the theater's history, stagehands and actors have reported spotting a woman in a white dress. She likes to hover stage right, at the top or bottom of an old spiral staircase.

Once, a stagehand asked what her name was.

She answered, "Marie."

An actress named Marie Cahill was a regular performer at the Fulton Opera House in her lifetime. Research concluded that the apparition must be Cahill, who died around the time that the theater started showing movies and films.

* * *

Mark was doing carpentry work in a stairwell that had been closed off for many years. He measured the space for the trim that he was cutting.

As he moved over to his miter saw, he suddenly sensed that he wasn't alone. Slowly, he looked up. A man in a light-colored suit and straw hat was moving toward him. Mark took a step back and nearly tripped over the saw's cord.

"Got a smoke?" asked the dapper man.

Before Mark could answer, the man disappeared.

Without wasting a moment, Mark ran from the theater and onto Prince Street. He stopped to catch his breath and promised to never set foot in the theater again, not even to finish his job.

Other theater employees have reported seeing the same ghost.

* * *

As if ghostly apparitions weren't enough, witnesses have reported hearing whistling and clapping coming from backstage.

The building was renovated in 1995. But prior to its renovation, the theater's gallery seating was closed to the public for safety concerns. Only movie-projector and spotlight operators were allowed in the area.

A university professor was running the spotlight for a show. She was surprised to see an older man sitting in the gallery, since it was off-limits. The professor approached the man.

"Do you have permission to be here?" she asked.

The man pointed to a young actress onstage. "That's my granddaughter. I'm here to watch her."

She certainly didn't want to be the one to kick an elderly man out of his seat. "Okay," she whispered. "Just be careful up here."

After the performance, she found herself beside the man's granddaughter. "I met your grandfather. Did he enjoy the show?"

The actress gave her a puzzled look. "Both of my grandfathers have passed. Neither of them ever saw me perform."

The professor thought for a moment before responding, "Well, maybe one has now."

The ghostly sightings at the Fulton Theatre are far from threatening. And if the venue provided an opportunity for a ghostly grandfather to finally watch his granddaughter perform onstage, it must be a pretty special place.

Katy's Church
Millville

S ometimes, a ghostly tale takes on a life of its own, growing a little each time the story is told. These stories can evolve into such fantastic retellings that it's difficult to know where the truth ends and the legends begin.

* * *

In Northeastern Pennsylvania, the borough of Millville was founded in 1772. The community was slow to grow. For years, the town was only accessible by the Native American trails that came together at Millville. As a result, the rural residents became self-sufficient.

In 1856, a road was constructed from Bloomsburg to LaPorte, sparking a growth spurt. It wasn't until 1887 that the railroad arrived and brought with it another small burst of growth. But even then, the town never grew much beyond its rural reputation.

When German immigrants brought with them the Lutheran religion, they needed places to worship.

The town's first Lutheran church was built and named the Immanuel Lutheran Church. Over the years, the church became known as Katy's Church.

* * *

The three girls sat in a circle next to the big tree. It was dark, and the summer sounds of chirping crickets and frogs added to the backdrop.

Maddie and Zoe came here whenever they were looking for a thrill, but it was Courtney's first visit to the cemetery next to Katy's church; she had just moved to the area with her family.

"Are either one of you going to tell me why we're sitting here?" asked Courtney.

"We had to wait until we got here," said Maddie. "It's much more dramatic to hear when you're sitting under the actual hanging tree."

Courtney glanced up at the tree as if seeing it for the first time.

Zoe held a flashlight under her chin to give her face an eerie glow. "According to some of the stories, Katy was a young, unmarried woman who became pregnant. She was ridiculed and shamed by everyone in town, so she hung herself from this tree."

"My turn!" Maddie held her own flashlight under her chin and continued. "Some say she was a young bride, and her beloved was a Civil War soldier who left her, got killed, and never returned. She was so sad that she hung herself right here."

"My favorite," said Zoe, "is the one where young Katy fell in love with a prominent rich, married man, and he got her pregnant."

Maggie picked up the storyline. "And then he used his name and reputation in the community to accuse her of being a witch. So all the townspeople formed a posse and dragged her from her bed and hung her from this tree."

"Why do all of these stories claim that she was pregnant?" laughed Courtney.

"Probably to make sure girls are too scared to have sex," giggled Zoe.

* * *

The reported paranormal activity that accompanies the legends includes phantom blood dripping from the windows of the church. A noose has been spotted, hanging from the tree where her life was supposedly taken. It is said that if you stand on Katy's grave and knock on the tree, her ghost will appear on the hill and start walking toward you.

Other sightings include an apparition walking the grounds in a white gown. Frequent reports also include strange lights and a voice calling out to visitors by their names. In addition, there are accounts of car trouble on the road. Finally, an unrelated tale talks about a pit on the property covered by a large rock. It's said that if you remove the boulder and drop a coin in the pit, you'll never hear it land.

In trying to uncover the truth behind the hauntings, the facts tell a different story. A widow, Catharine (Katy) Vandine was devoted to both her faith and her community. In the community's time of need, this mother of five donated land for the construction of the town's first Lutheran church. Katy herself attended services there until her death in 1899 at the age of 87. It didn't take long before everyone in town began to call the place of worship Katy's Church. She was buried there, in what is now known as Katy Vandine's Cemetery.

Obviously, the stories of a teenage Katy dying by suicide are not true. However, the community could have publicly shamed a young girl for getting pregnant out of wedlock or having an affair with a married man. It's also possible that they took matters into their own hands if she was accused of being a witch.

Rumors aren't always without a certain element of truth. There might have been some foundation on which these stories have grown. Katy was a beloved community member, and her devotion to her faith and community earned her a legacy namesake. But maybe other souls haunt this graveyard. Perhaps they are looking for acknowledgment that they existed.

Hershey Hotel, Factory, and Park
Hershey

As a young man, Milton Hershey was known for his convictions, curiosity, and willingness to take great risks. He was only 26 years old and completely broke, having spent every penny on two failed candy businesses. But Hershey had a dream to mass-produce an affordable milk chocolate that could be available to everyone.

After a trial-and-error process, he was so successful that his operations outgrew his facility in Lancaster. He searched for a good location to build a new factory. He chose a rural location in the isolated countryside. While his advisors deemed the location too remote, Hershey saw a steady supply of milk and hardworking German immigrants. Hershey also had a dream of creating an entirely new community—a "model" town.

By 1905, laborers built a factory, housing, schools, and businesses. The town also had a volunteer fire department and a YMCA. A trolley system and utilities served the town's population. Land was set aside for Hershey Park, which opened on May 30, 1906.

The park became its own attraction, drawing tourists from throughout the state. On July 4, 1908, the park got its first ride: a merry-go-round that was later upgraded to a carousel. In 1911, a pool opened.

In 1931, in the midst of the Great Depression, Milton Hershey created new jobs for the people in his community. He decided to build a grand hotel. With 170 rooms for guests; 22 rooms for servants; a garage for 100 cars; and multiple dining rooms, ballrooms, and parlors, Hotel Hershey opened in May of 1933.

* * *

Guests have spotted a ghostly Mr. Hershey at both the hotel and in the park. Sightings are often accompanied by a strong smell of cigar smoke. At Hotel Hershey, doors have been known to open and close on their own. Footsteps are frequently heard in the wine cellar, and other unexplained noises are heard throughout the building.

Not all the sightings are assumed to be Hershey. One guest reported that her skirt was inexplicably tugged when no one was there to tug on it. Another guest reported that the apparition of a little boy appeared in her polaroid photo. Night employees have seen a shadow darting across the hall on the third floor.

Another dark shadow has been spotted near the roller coaster, where a worker tragically lost his life.

People also report seeing children, wearing their old-fashioned bathing suits, in an area where the pool used to be. Even the park's carousel is said to be haunted.

* * *

The security guard meandered casually down the path that he'd walked a hundred times before. He liked his job. There were worse places than Hershey Park to wander around at night. Knowing how busy the park was during the day, he liked being there when it was quiet, after the guests had gone home, their bellies full of sugar and their senses overstimulated by a day of crowds and thrill rides.

As he rounded the corner and the carousel came into view, the lights flashed on, and he jumped back, startled. The horses started to turn, and the music blared into the quiet night. His senses on high alert, the guard approached slowly, his hand on his weapon.

"Who's there?" he shouted.

No one answered.

He moved around to the control booth, his eyes scanning for any movement. There was nothing to explain how the ride had begun operating, seemingly all by itself.

He turned the ride off, bringing the park back to quiet. The silence seemed eerie after the unexplained interruption. Breathing a sigh of relief, the guard started to walk away.

Behind him, the ride came aglow once again.

Spinning around, the guard locked his eyes on the control booth. A dark, shadowy figure stood by the ride's controls.

The guard hurried toward the intruder. But before he reached the control panel, the figure had vanished.

Gettysburg Battlefield
Gettysburg

Some ghosts appear as a result of tragedy. Others seem to come to prevent it. If legend is true, Gettysburg Battlefield has been home to both types of paranormal encounters.

On July 1, 1863, the bloodiest battle of the Civil War began in Gettysburg, with the first shots ringing out in the early morning hours. It was a battle of "brothers against brothers." The majority of the soldiers were under the age of 30. Some children as young as 12 served as drummer boys or buglers. Regardless of age, each person came prepared to die for their cause but prayed they wouldn't have to.

For three days, the sounds of gunfire, explosions, and screams of the injured and dying filled the air. Soldiers fought the battle at close range, charging toward one another in hails of gunfire. In some attacks, hundreds of men were killed in minutes, their lives cut short by cannonballs, bullets, swords, and bayonets.

With bedrock just below the soil's surface, soldiers were unable to dig trenches. The generally flat field made the rock formations of Devil's Den a highly sought source of cover. Because of this, the land surrounding this outcropping of rocks was one of the bloodiest areas of the entire battlefield.

On July 3, 1863, the Confederate troops were forced to retreat. The price was paid with the lives of more than 50,000 souls. Photographs taken after the battle show the land covered with the bodies of fallen soldiers. The grim task of burying the dead began in the early evening hours of July 4.

Most bodies were buried where they fell, often in mass graves, just 10 to 18 inches below the surface. The corpses, left in the hot sun for days, were in advanced states of decomposition. Men working in the burial parties recalled that many of the bodies simply fell apart as they landed in the graves. Some Confederate bodies were simply covered with brush and rock, leaving them exposed to the elements and animals. It took more than a week to inter all the soldiers.

In addition to the men who'd died in battle, the bodies of nearly 5,000 fallen horses and mules were left scattered across the field. Moving them for burial would have been extremely difficult, so they were set on fire. Between the burning horses and decomposing soldiers, the stench of death was strong; it's said that people could smell Gettysburg 40 miles in all directions. The stench lingered for months.

The corpses bloated, and rain softened the earth. As time passed, people in Gettysburg reported seeing arms or legs of corpses, blackened by decay, poking out of the ground.

Although an attempt was later made to recover the bodies from those mass graves—and some were ultimately buried properly—a large number of soldiers remained unidentified. Not all mass graves were found, leaving many men in unmarked graves scattered across the battlefield.

Today, Gettysburg Battlefield is a national park. Visitors can hike pathways, observe monuments, and climb on the Devil's Den boulder formation. Names of the fallen, along with their regiment numbers, carved into the rocks by their fellow soldiers, are still visible.

As late as 1996, corpses of soldiers were still being found after heavy rains and erosion exposed their remains. It's possible that such discoveries will continue for generations to come.

* * *

Shawn checked his watch. He and his girlfriend had been hiking around the Valley of Death between Devil's Den and Little Round Top for the last several hours.

"We should get back to the campground," he said.

It was going to be dark soon, and they had a 2-mile hike back to their tent.

"Sounds good," said his girlfriend. "Even if we missed all the re-enactments this year, I'm glad we got to see Little Round Top."

"I agree," said Shawn. "It's been a great trip."

They walked in silence for a few minutes, but the still air was interrupted by the eerie notes of someone playing "Taps" on a bugle.

"Do you hear that?" Shawn asked.

"Where's it coming from?"

Shawn pointed. "I think the woods over there."

They studied the trees, trying to identify the source of the sound.

"Do you see that?" exclaimed Shawn.

A thin white mist formed along the treeline. Several soldiers, appearing from nowhere, walked out from the woods.

* * *

It was a typical evening when the man drove with his uncle through Gettysburg National Military Park. While they'd heard ghost stories associated with the area, they weren't looking for a paranormal encounter. But as they drove along the road, a light fog rolled in, giving the otherwise clear evening an ominous feel.

"Do you hear that?" the man asked his uncle.

"It sounds like people are moving out there on my side of the car," his uncle replied.

"I hear it coming from my side too," the man said.

Somewhere in the buzz of crickets and other bugs, strange noises, like the rush of movement, were coming from all directions. The sounds were barely perceptible, but both men were certain they heard them.

The man's uncle pulled out a mobile phone and began recording. It was then that they saw movement. Almost translucent humanoid shapes were rushing across the grassy field.

The two men drove slowly in silence as they watched the strange figures move.

When their vehicle exited the park, the eerie fog was gone, and the strange sights and sounds ceased.

Later, when they watched the recording, they were relieved to have captured on film what they had witnessed.

Paranormal activity was already being reported on and around Gettysburg Battlefield shortly after the battle ended. It seems the spirits of the determined soldiers were restless from the start.

Perhaps the most intriguing haunting associated with the Gettysburg Battlefield came during the battle. Colonel Joshua Chamberlain had led his men of the 20th Maine regiment toward Gettysburg in a mad dash to help their Union brothers. They were far behind and pushed quickly through the oppressive summer heat as fast as they could.

When they came to a fork in the road, they were unsure which way to go. Choosing the wrong path would have prevented them from joining the fight. As Chamberlain and his troops assessed the situation, a mysterious man rode up to them in the moonlight on a pale horse. The man wore what was described as a brightly colored tricorn hat.

The strange man and his horse proceeded down one of the roads, then motioned toward Chamberlain and his men to follow. So they did. They followed the man all the way to the Union battlelines, where they quickly joined the fight.

Perhaps the strange man would have been forgotten by the 20th Maine regiment. The soldiers were fighting for their lives and their country. But as the men stood in a vital tactical position at Little Round Top, pushing back the Confederate soldiers with heavy fire at close range, they ran out of ammunition.

Chamberlain and his men had little choice. Retreat would have cost the Union its position and could have changed the outcome of the battle. He told the regiment to ready their bayonets; they would have to charge into the heart of the Confederate forces and fight.

As Chamberlain's soldiers prepared to charge forward, frightened by the reality that this fight could be their last, they once again saw the man with the brightly colored tricorn hat. It's said that he stood in front of the Union line, holding a flaming sword. This time, there was no mistaking that the man before them was none other than George Washington, who had been dead for more than 60 years.

Inspired by the specter of their nation's first president, the men charged forward, a move that seemed to shock the Confederate troops, who recoiled from the attack. Not only did the members of the 20th Maine regiment hold their position, but they were also able to capture several Confederate soldiers as they fled in a panicked retreat.

Chamberlain himself later spoke of the incident saying, ". . . who among us can say that such a thing was impossible? We have not yet sounded or explored the immortal life that lies out beyond the Bar . . . I only know the effect, but I dare not explain or deny the cause."

Who could say it better than that? Humankind does not understand the mysteries of death or what comes after it. So, when a spirit presents itself, whether to protect or remind humanity of the past, one should accept and respect the awe of it without feeling compelled to explain it.

Gettysburg College
Gettysburg

There are moments in time that are so traumatic that the events are basically sealed away. But every now and then, a moment is unlocked, and people find themselves standing in the midst of it exactly as it unfolded so long ago. This phenomenon has been experienced time and again throughout Gettysburg, in locations ranging from battlefields to field hospitals, including on the campus of Gettysburg College.

* * *

Gettysburg College was founded in 1832. When the Battle of Gettysburg erupted in 1863, the college stood in the heart of warfare.

On that first day of fighting, Pennsylvania Hall was turned into a field hospital. Today, the hall serves as an administrative office, but in 1863, it was a dormitory. With the battlefield adjacent to campus, the large building seemed like an ideal place to treat hundreds of severely wounded men. Both Union and Confederate soldiers were brought into the makeshift hospital, where their wounds were crudely treated without the benefit of pain medication or sterile tools.

Students from the college were quick to provide aid to soldiers. Hallways and rooms soon filled with bloodied young men. One student reported that no matter where they were on campus, they could hear the cries and prayers of the wounded and dying.

Piles of amputated limbs were carried out of the building as doctors fought to provide the best treatment they could, given their limited resources. Many soldiers died from blood loss and shock as their bodies were hacked apart in an attempt to save them. The dormitory, which just days before had been a place to study and rest, was filled with unimaginable agony, despair, and death. Although the battle would be over in just three days, its impact would be felt long after the war ended.

* * *

Given this connection with the Battle of Gettysburg, it's no wonder the campus of Gettysburg College is notoriously haunted. And it's not surprising that Pennsylvania Hall is a paranormal hotspot. Accounts include people hearing the cries and moans of young soldiers in agony. Others report apparitions of soldiers standing guard, some even waving at passersby.

One particularly chilling account comes from the 1980s, when two administrators were working late one evening.

"What a day," Shirley said. She entered the elevator and pushed the button for the ground floor.

Jane was too tired to speak; she just nodded her agreement, glad to be going home.

The elevator bypassed their requested stop and continued to the lower level, where it came to rest in the basement.

"What's going on?" Jane asked.

"I have no idea," Shirley replied.

As the doors slowly opened, the women were met with a horrifying scene.

The basement floor, usually cluttered with items set aside for storage, was filled with bloody Civil War soldiers. Doctors rushed to work on them, some amputating injured limbs with bone saws, as the men cried out in agony.

One of the medical assistants turned and looked at the women, then began walking toward them with outstretched arms.

"Push the button," shouted Jane.

"I'm trying," said Shirley.

The elevator doors closed, and the elevator began its ascent. When the women arrived on the first floor, they rushed to the security officer.

After telling him what they'd seen, they agreed to go back with him to investigate. But this time, when the doors opened, an ordinary basement storage scene was revealed.

Whatever time-slip had taken place, it was over.

Jennie Wade House
Gettysburg

Mary Virginia Wade, known to her friends and family as Jennie, was just 17 years old when the Civil War began in 1861. No one could have imagined that the war would rage on for nearly four years. When the Confederate army advanced on Gettysburg on July 1, 1863, the community was showered in bullets and bathed in blood.

It's difficult to imagine the collective fear that gripped the community between July 1 and July 4, 1863. Civilians were hunkered down in their homes. Some of those homes became field hospitals, with young men sometimes dying on the front lawns while others had limbs amputated atop dining room tables.

Before the battle began, Jennie's mother, Mary, had gone to be with her oldest daughter, Georgia, who had given birth to a baby boy just days before the Confederates arrived. Worried that their home would be too dangerous to stay in, Jennie took her two younger brothers and a neighbor boy, Isaac, to Georgia's place, where they felt they would be safer.

It wasn't long before the duplex Georgia lived in was at the heart of the battle. Jennie remained calm, despite the chaos around her. She and her mother tended to Georgia and the newborn, while doing all they could to help the Union troops by supplying them with bread and water.

On the morning of July 3, Jennie began her day by reading scriptures, as she always did. Then she spoke briefly with her sister Georgia, who was in a bed set up in the parlor, with her newborn son.

With all the fighting going on around them, the women were naturally worried. Jennie told her sister, "If anyone is to die in this house today, I hope it is me for, Georgia, you have that little baby."

With those words, she opened the door to the kitchen, adjacent to the parlor, and prepared more bread for the troops. Leaving the parlor door open, Jennie stood behind it—an extra layer of protection in case a stray bullet should hit the home. As Jennie stood in the corner of the kitchen, kneading dough, her mother stoked the fire nearby.

At approximately 8:30 a.m., a bullet crashed through the outside door of the kitchen, ripped through the parlor door, and tore into Jennie's upper back. It pierced her heart, killing her almost instantly.

Mary's screams drew the attention of Union soldiers who had been upstairs. They rushed to the kitchen to find Jennie dead on the floor.

Bullets peppered the brick home. One came through the parlor window and lodged into the bedpost not far from Georgia and her baby. An artillery shell came through the roof of the home, ripping a hole in the wall between the two sides of the duplex.

The soldiers knew they had to get the family out of the house. However, every exit would take them directly into the line of fire. They gathered the family and hurried upstairs. Using the butts of their rifles, they enlarged the hole from the shell that had come through the roof. Georgia, her newborn, and the boys were able to squeeze through the hole, hurry through the neighbors' home, run out the back of the house, and scurry into the cellar.

When the soldiers realized that Mary was not with them, two ran back to the kitchen. They found her cradling Jennie's lifeless body. They gathered a quilt, wrapped Jennie in it, and carried her to the cellar. The family hid in the basement for 18 hours as bullets continued to rain through the home above them. Before the day was done, more than 150 bullets had hit the house.

The Confederate troops retreated the next day, and Jennie's body was buried in the garden behind the house on July 4. That day, Mary finished what Jennie had started. She prepared 15 loaves of bread with the dough that her beloved daughter had been kneading, and she fed the Union troops.

Although the number of soldiers killed during the Battle of Gettysburg is estimated to be more than 50,000, Jennie was the only civilian who died in the crossfire. Her body was moved twice before she found her final resting place in the Evergreen Cemetery.

In 1900, a monument was erected at her gravesite, and a perpetual American flag flies beside her tombstone.

She is one of only two women in the US with such an honor. The other is Betsy Ross.

Nearly 20 years after Jennie's death, her mother was given a pension from the US Senate. They determined that Jennie was killed while serving the Union. She tended to the troops, making sure they had food and water; she was, after all, making bread for them when she died. She served her country and sadly paid the ultimate price for her loyalty.

Today, the home where Jennie Wade was killed is a historical museum. Visitors can step into the past and learn about Jennie's life and untimely death. The walls and doors are still riddled with bullet holes, including holes from the bullet that took her life.

Artifacts on display in the home include the shell that burst through the roof; a piece of wood from the original kitchen floor, stained with Jennie's blood; and the dough tray Jennie was using the moment she died.

* * *

The two women stood just outside the door, gazing at the bullet hole.

"At the time of her death, Jennie was betrothed to her childhood friend Jonston "Jack" Skelly," the tour guide said. "Just before Jennie died, Jack was wounded in a battle and taken captive. He died from his wounds on July 12, 1863, just nine days after Jennie. Neither knew of the other's passing."

"That's so sad," one of the women said quietly.

"Is it true that people who put their finger through the bullet hole in the door will get engaged?" the other asked the tour guide.

"We regularly receive letters and emails from couples, claiming they are proof that the legend is true. Many believe kind-hearted Jennie wants others to experience the joy of being married, which she was denied."

The women, along with the rest of their small group, followed the guide into the home.

"I've heard this place is haunted," a boy on the tour remarked.

"We've had numerous reports of paranormal activity throughout the house," the guide replied. "Some accounts include full-body apparitions, people being touched by unseen hands, orbs, unexplained tapping sounds, and footsteps. Many believe that in addition to Jennie's spirit, which seems comforting to those who are feeling anxious or afraid, some of the soldiers who were here when Jennie died were so affected by her passing that they've chosen to stay. We think they're guarding the home in their afterlife."

The group made their way upstairs, listening intently as the guide shared the history of each space. Then, when everyone else went back down the steps to the next portion of the tour, the two women lagged behind, snapping a few pictures.

One of them gasped. "Oh my gosh, look at this."

She held up her phone, and her friend gazed at the image on it. The shadow figure of a woman in period dress was reflected in the mirror over the wash basin. The women glanced down the hallway in the direction of the figure. The hallway was empty.

Bibliography

PREFACE

History.com Editors. *"Pennsylvania."* (history.com).
June 13, 2022

"Native American Tribes of Pennsylvania." Native
American Languages (native-languages.org). Accessed
December 26, 2023.

"Why and How Were the Quakers Persecuted?"
Youth Quake Now: Radical Faith & Activism
(youthquakenow.com). Access December 26, 2023.

EASTERN STATE PENITENTIARY *(Philadelphia)*

Belanger, Jeff and Nick Groff and Zak Bagans (writers),
and Zak Bagans and Nick Groff (directors). "Eastern
State Penitentiary." *Ghost Adventures* (Season 2:
Episode 6). July 10, 2009.

Dalrymple, Laurel. "Is Eastern State Penitentiary Really
Haunted?" NPR News (npr.org). October 24, 2013.

Janofsky, Jennifer Lawrence. "Eastern State
Penitentiary." The Encyclopedia of Greater
Philadelphia (philadelphiaencyclopedia.org).
Accessed December 26, 2023.

"Eastern State Haunted History." Travel Channel
(travelchannel.com). Accessed December 28, 2023.

"History of Corrections—Punishment, Prevention, or
Rehabilitation?" Encyclopedia.Com (encyclopedia.com).
Accessed December 26, 2023.

OLD JAIL MUSEUM *(Jim Thorpe)*

"History." Old Jail Museum (theoldjailmuseum.com).
Accessed March 17, 2024.

Pirro, J.F. "Preserving the History of the
Molly Maguires." Lehigh Valley Marketplace
(lehighvalleymarketplace.com). Accessed
March 19, 2024.

Schumm, Laura. "Who Were the Molly Maguires?" History (history.com). August 19, 2018.

Staff Reporter. "Weissport Man Gets Weekends Jail Sentence." *Jim Thorpe Times News*. September 29, 1966.

PENNHURST STATE SCHOOL AND HOSPITAL
(Spring City)

AP. "Workers Indicted in Patient Abuse." *The New York Times*. November 4, 1983.

Katovitch, Diana M. "Who Should Tell the Story? The Pennhurst Haunted Asylum and the Pennhurst Museum in Public History." National Council on Public History (ncph.org). June 7, 2022.

"About Pennhurst State School and Hospital." Pennhurst Memorial & Preservation Alliance (preservepennhurst.org). Access January 12, 2024.

Tarabay, Jamie. "Haunted House Has Painful Past as Asylum." NPR News (npr.org). October 29, 2010.

Taylor, Jodi Alexander (director). "Pennhurst." (film). March 2023.

DIXMONT STATE HOSPITAL *(Pittsburg)*

"History." dixmonthospital.com (dixmonthospital .com). Access February 17, 2024.

Northwood, Arlisha R. "Dorthea Dix (1802-1887)." National Women's History Museum (womenshistory .org). 2017.

Paranormal in Pennsylvania. "Soul Sentinels of the Morgue." YouTube (youtube.com). March 16, 2023.

Snedden, Jeffrey. "The ghosts of Dixmont, the history of St. Ann Catholic Church." *The Times* (timesonline.com). October 25, 2016.

HARRISBURG STATE HOSPITAL *(Harrisburg)*

Dubs, Gerald. "Murder suspect 'extra quiet' night of killing." *The Evening Sun*. September 23, 1982.

"City on the Hill" (hsh.thoms-industries.com) Accessed February 24, 2024.

Staff Writer. "DA Would Drop Murder Charge." *Public Opinion*. January 28, 1965.

Staff Writer. "Insane Patient Kills Physician." *Messenger-Inquirer*. January 8, 1930.

Staff Writer. "Mrs. Heyneman is judged insane by commission." *The Gazette and Daily*. Dec 30, 1947.

Staff Writer. "Second Slaying Probed: Youth Held in Mother's Death." *York Daily Record*. May 5, 1973.

Staff Writer. "West Fairview Grocer, Held on Serious Offense, Found Insane Awaiting Trial." *The Sentinel*. January 5, 1935.

HILL VIEW MANOR *(New Castle)*

Blogger in Philly Ghosts. "Haunted Hill View Manor." Philly Ghosts (phillyghosts.com). Accessed February 19, 2024.

Braden, Beth. "Haunted History: A Shuttered Pennsylvania Nursing Home is Home to Dozens of Trapped Souls." Travel Channel (travelchannel.com). Accessed February 19, 2024.

Lucy, Mina. "Hill View Manor's Dark Past: Uncovering Forgotten Tragedies and Paranormal Activity." Mina Lucy Blog (minalucy.com). Accessed February 19, 2024.

Mick. "Hill View Manor – New Castle, Pa." Pennsylvania Mounts of Attractions (pennsylvania-mountains-of-attractions.com). Accessed February 19, 2024.

"Haunted Hill View Manor." Haunted Hill View Manor (hauntedhillviewmanor.com). Accessed February 19, 2024.

Roknick, Michael. "Spirits, investigators now roam halls of former care home." *The Herald* (sharonherald.com). October 31, 2020.

BETSY ROSS HOUSE *(Philadelphia)*

Alexander, Kerri Lee. "Betsy Ross." National Women's History Museum (womenshistory.org). Accessed March 18, 2024.

Brady, Amanda. "Haunted History: Betsy Ross House highlights the gruesome realities of living in 18th century." ABC 7 News (acb7news.com). October 25, 2022.

Glessner, Rusty. "Exploring the Betsy Ross House in Philadelphia." PA Bucket List (pabucketlist.com). Accessed March 18, 2024.

Pauper, Anneliese. "Betsy Ross House." Paranormal (and True Crime) (pennsylvaniaparanormal.tumblr.com). January 29, 2016.

Amber. "The Besty Ross House." Philly Ghosts (phillyghosts.com). Accessed March 18, 2024.

"Betsy Ross House." Historic Philadelphia, Inc. (historicphiladelphia.org). Accessed March 18, 2024.

"The Betsy Ross House Offers Plenty of Horrors on its Halloween Tours. And it's All True." *The Philadelphia Inquirer* (inquirer.com). October 23, 2022.

"The Betsy Ross House." US History.org (ushistory.org). Accessed March 18, 2024.

"A Brief Biography of Betsy Ross." US History.org (ushistory.org). Accessed March 18, 2024.

SAYRE MANSION *(Bethlehem)*

Aughtry, Ryan (producer). "The Sayre Specters." *Ghost Hunters* (Season 15, Episode 8). November 19, 2022.

Whelan, Frank. "A Grand Beginning: Fountain Hill was once the address of choice for the Valley's elite." *The Morning Call.* July 01, 1990.

Whelan, Frank. "Industrialist Sayre's diaries are historic treasure trove." *The Morning Call.* January 20, 1985.

GONDER MANSION & STRASBURG CEMETERY *(Strasburg)*

"About Strasburg…Our History." Strasburg, Pennsylvania (strasburgpa.com). Accessed January 21, 2024.

"The Restless Spirit of Annie Gonder." *The Pennsylvania Rambler* (thepennsylvaniaramber.com). June 11, 2023.

"The Story Behind This Haunted Cemetery in Pennsylvania is Terrifying." Travel Maven (original.newsbreak.com). June 30, 2023.

Price-Williams, Beth. "The Story Behind This Haunted Cemetery in Pennsylvania Will Chill You to the Bone." Only In Your State (onlyinyourstate.com). November 25, 2021.

Unchartedadam. "Laughing Ghost of Gonder Mansion." Uncharted Lancaster (unchartedlancaster.com). October 29, 2019.

GRAEME PARK *(Horsham)*

"Dr. Thomas Graeme." Find a Grave (findagrave.com). Accessed March 20, 2024.

"Elizabeth Graeme Fergusson." History of American Women (womenhistoryblog.com). Accessed March 23, 2024.

"Halloween Tours & Stories." Graeme Park (graemepark.org). Accessed March 21, 2024.

"History." Graeme Park (graemepark.org). Accessed March 20, 2024.

"Is Graeme Park Haunted?" Graeme Park (graemepark.org). Accessed March 20, 2024.

KING GEORGE II INN *(Bristol)*

Martin, Erich. "Tales Of Ghosts Continue To Haunt Historic Bristol Restaurant." Levittownnow.com (levittownnow.com) October 30, 2017.

Murphy. "King George II Inn (Bristol, PA)." Journey With Murphy (journeywithmurphy.com). August 22, 2020.

"About Us." Historic King George II Inn (kginn.com). Accessed February 14, 2024.

"King George II Inn." Haunted Places (hauntedplaces .org). Accessed February 18, 2024.

"King George II Inn." Tour Bristol Borough (tourbristol .org). Accessed February 18, 2024.

HARMONY INN *(Harmony)*

Allegheny Paranormal. "The Haunting of Harmony Inn – What's Buried in the Walls?!" YouTube (youtube.com). September 10, 2023.

Butler Eagle. "Haunted History of Butler County: The Harmony Inn." YouTube (youtube.com). October 31, 2023.

Grubbs, Paula. "Harmony Inn potentially haunted by numerous entities." *Butler Eagle* (butlereagle.com). October 31, 2023.

"Harmony, Pennsylvania: Harmony Inn." HauntedHouses.com (hauntedhouses.com). Access January 28, 2024.

"History of Harmony." Harmony Museum (harmonymuseum.org). Accessed January 28, 2024.

"The Harmony Inn." North Country Brewing Company (northcountrybrewing.com). Accessed January 28, 2024.

BRINTON LODGE *(Chester & Philadelphia Counties)*

Bechtel, Ali. "A Storied Past & Crafty Present: The Brinton Lodge." Berks County Living (berkscountyliving.com). February 4, 2019.

Claypoole, Spencer. "History of North Coventry Township." North Coventry Township (northcovertrytownship.com). February 10, 2024.

Godshalk, Dutch. "Ghost tours, spooky stories, and murder mysteries about this Halloween season." *The Mercury* (pottsmerc.com). September 23, 2021.

"Brinton Lodge." Brinton Lodge (brintonlodge.com). Accessed February 10, 2024.

"Brinton's Lodge." This Haunted Place (thishauntedplace.com). Accessed February 10, 2024.

"Martin Urner." Find A Grave (findagrave.com). Accessed February 11, 2024.

"The Schuylkill Canal: The Canal's Past." The Schuylkill Canal Association (schuylkillcanal.org). Accessed February 11, 2024.

Speros, Susan. "Foundations: Some say the past walks the halls at Brinton Lodge." *Reading Eagle* (readingeagle.com). August 19, 2021.

Meder, Amanda Linette. "The Brinton Lodge Ghost Tour Review." Amanda Linette Meder (amandalinettemeder.com). October 25, 2019.

HOTEL BETHLEHEM *(Bethlehem)*

Amber. "Haunted Hotel Bethlehem." Civil War Ghosts (civilwarghosts.com). Accessed March 3, 2024.

"Historic Hotel Bethlehem: Ghost Stories." Historic Hotels (historichotels.org). Accessed March 3, 2024.

"Historic Hotel Bethlehem: History." Historic Hotels (historichotels.org). Accessed March 3, 2024.

"Historic Moravian Bethlehem Story." Historic Bethlehem Museums & Sites (historicbethlehem.org). Accessed March 3, 2024.

BUBE'S BREWERY *(Mount Joy)*

Anderson, Akil (story producer) and Alan David (executive director). "A Family of Spirits." *Ghost Hunters* (Season 8, Episode 9). April 25, 2012.

Molitoris, Cathy. "Digging Into History." *Town Lively* (townlively.com). October 6, 2021.

Shenk, Rochelle. "'Ghost Hunters' investigate Bube's Brewery." Lancaster Online (lancasteronlin.com). March 5, 2012.

Stairiker, Kevin. "After more than two centuries, Bubes brewery still lives up to Alois vision." LPN: Lancaster Online (lancasteronlin.com). August 15, 2018.

Stauffer, Cindy and Dan Nephin. "Spirits of another kind at Bube's Brewery." LPN: Lancaster Online (lancasteronlin.com). April 25, 2012.

Wagner, Rich. "History of Bube's Brewery." Zymurgy (pabreweryhistorians.tripod.com). Spring 1984.

Wright, Mary Ellen. "Bube's Brewery in Mount Joy offers glimpse into history, plus varied kinds of entertainment." LPN: Lancaster Online (lancasteronline.com). April 9, 2017.

MISHLER THEATRE *(Altoona)*

Amber. "Mishler Theatre." Civil War Ghosts (civilwarghosts.com). Accessed February 11, 2024.

"About the Horseshoe Curve." Railroaders Memorial Museum (railroadcity.org). Accessed February 11, 2024.

"Charles Mishler Historical Marker." ExplorePAHistory. com (explorepahistory.com). Accessed February 11, 2024.

"Haunted Mishler Theatre: 12 Year Old Tells Her Ghostly Tale." Pennsylvania Mountains of Attractions (pennsylvania-mountains-of-attractions.com). Accessed February 11, 2024.

"History." Mishler Theatre (mischlertheatre.org). Accessed January 28, 2024.

"History of Altoona." City of Altoona (altoonapa.gov). Accessed February 11, 2024.

Zeak, Matthew. "The Mishler: Blair County's Historic Playhouse." Pennsylvania Center for the Book (pabook. libraries.psu.edu). Fall 2010.

FULTON THEATRE *(Lancaster)*

"History." Fulton Theatre (thefulton.org). Accessed January 20, 2024.

"Robert Fulton." National Inventors Hall of Fame (invent.org). Accessed January 20, 2024.

"Secrets of the Theatre." Fulton Theatre (thefulton.org). Accessed January 20, 2024.

KATY'S CHURCH *(Millville)*

Charnoff, Amber. "Haunted Pennsylvania. Most haunted spots in the keystone state." ABC 27 (abc27.com). October 8, 2023.

Farenish, Melissa. "The haunted legend of Katy's Church in Millville." NorthcentralPA.com (northcentralpa.com). October 29, 2021.

Meristem, Woody. "Katy's Church." In Forest and Field (forestandfield.blogspot.com). March 17, 2021.

"Catharine Poust Vandine." Find a Grave (findagrave. com). Accessed January 13, 2024.

"Katy's church immortalized by woodworker Herman Jones." *The Daily Item* (dailyitem.com). August 22, 2014.

Pauper, Anneliese. "Katy's Church." Paranormal (and True Crime) (pennsylvaniaparanormal.tumblr.com). October 13, 2017.

Shetler, May. "Katys Church The Real Story." MayCris Photo Artists (outhousesoutandabout.com). Accessed January 15, 2024.

HERSHEY PARK *(Hershey)*

Cassidy, Pamela and Eliza Harrison. "One Man's Vision: Hershey A Model Town, 1988." The Hershey Story (hersheystory.org). Accessed January 27, 2024.

"All 7 Pennsylvania chocolate factory explosion victims found." AP (apnews.com). March 27, 2023.

"DA: Pa. dad took kids to theme park before killing family, self." CBS News (cbsnews.com). August 15, 2016.

"Hershey Chronology." Hershey Community Archives (hersheyarchives.org). Accessed January 28, 2024.

"History of the Hotel Hershey." The Hotel Hershey (thehotelhershey.com). Accessed January 28, 2024.

"Lancaster Caramel Company." Hershey Community Archives (hersheyarchives.org). September 6, 2018.

"Milton S. Hershey and the RMS Titanic." Hershey Community Archives (hersheyarchives.org). March 18, 2020.

"Milton S. Hershey: The Man Who Started It All." The Hershey Story (hersheystory.org). Accessed January 27, 2024.

"Origins of Hershey's Milk Chocolate." Hershey Community Archives (hersheyarchibes.org). June 3, 2021.

"The Hotel Hershey." Haunted Places (hauntedplaces
.org). Accessed January 28, 2024.

TheresaHPIR. "The Ghosts of Hershey Park."
Theresa's Haunted History of the Tri-State
(theresashauntedhistoryofthetri-state.blogspot.com).
April 24, 2014.

Wolf, Christopher E. *Ghosts of Hershey and Vicinity*.
Atglen, PA: Schiffer Publishing. April, 2009.

GETTYSBURG BATTLEFIELD *(Gettysburg)*
"History: An Overview." Gettysburg, Pennsylvania
(gettysburgpa.gov). Accessed March 2, 2024.

Lincoln, Abraham. "Gettysburg Address." Library of
Congress (loc.gov). November 19, 1863.

Henry, M.B. "A Ghost at Gettysburg: The 20th Maine's
Mysterious Encounter." M.B. Henry (mb-henry.com).
July 11, 2018.

"Gettysburg." American Battlefield Trust (battlefields
.org). Accessed March 1, 2024.

"Man captures Gettysburg 'ghosts' in spine-tingling
video during tour of Civil War site." (fox5dc.com).
September 16, 2020.

The UnXplained Zone. "Haunted History: Ghosts of
Gettysburg (s1, E2) | Full Episode." YouTube (youtube
.com). November 20, 2021.

Ward, Allie. "Burying the Dead." The Gettysburg
Compiler: On the Front Lines of History
(gettysburgcompiler.org). February 8, 2012

GETTYSBURG COLLEGE *(Gettysburg)*
Henry, M.B. "A Ghost at Gettysburg: Pennsylvania Hall
and Civil War Medicine." M.B. Henry (mb-henry.com).
October 21, 2019.

"Abraham Lincoln's Gettysburg Address."
American Battlefield Trust (battlefields.org).
Accessed March 2, 2024.

"College History." Gettysburg College (Gettysburg.edu).
Accessed March 2, 2024.

Penrose, Isabel Gibson. "Haunted G-Burg: the paranormal pervades campus." *The Gettysburgian* (gettsyburgian.com). November 3, 2014.

Zimmerman, Noelle. "The Spirits of Stevens Hall." *The Gettsyburgian* (gettsyburgian.com). November 18, 2017.

JENNIE WADE HOUSE *(Gettysburg)*
Belanger, Jeff (writer), Zak Baggans (director) & Nick Groff (director). "Gettysburg" (Season 4 Episode 1). September 17, 2010.

"Gettysburg Battlefield Bus Tours." (gettysburgbattlefieldtours.com). Accessed February 25, 2024.

"The Jennie Wade House." (civilwarghosts.com) Accessed February 25, 2024.

About Jessica Freeburg

Jessica Freeburg is an internationally published author, history nerd, and researcher of the unexplained. She has written a variety of books, ranging from graphic novels to paranormal fiction and nonfiction focused on creepy legends and dark moments from history.

As the founder of Ghost Stories Ink, Jessica has performed paranormal investigations at reportedly haunted locations across the US. She has appeared in documentaries and shows on such networks as the Travel Channel and Amazon Prime—talking about ghosts and haunted places—and can often be heard cohosting the wildly popular podcast *Darkness Radio*.

You can learn more about her work at www.jessicafreeburg.com.

About Natalie Fowler

Natalie Fowler, once a practicing attorney, is now an award-winning author and ghost writer. Her published works include nonfiction books on poignant—and sometimes dark—historical events and haunting legends.

She is the researcher and historian for Ghost Stories Ink and has led paranormal investigations at some of the most notoriously haunted locations in the country. Inspired by the concept of spirit rescue, she cofounded a paranormal group called Paranormal Services Cooperative and has published accounts of her work as a medium in this field. You can learn more about her work and publications at www.nataliefowler.com.

True Tales of Bigfoot, Vampires, and Other Legendary Creatures

Monsters of the Northeast
Jessica Freeburg & Natalie Fowler

Monsters of the Northeast:
True Tales of Bigfoot, Vampires, and Other Legendary Creatures

Jessica Freeburg & Natalie Fowler

ISBN: 978-1-64755-443-9 • $9.95 • 5 x 8
paperback • 160 pages

Vampires prey upon families from beyond the grave. A monstrous dog vanishes into thin air. A red-eyed beast terrorizes homeowners while helping itself to beloved pets—for dinner. The Northeast's history includes several unimaginable encounters with legendary creatures. This collection of stories presents the creepiest, most surprising monsters ever seen in the Northeast. Horror fans and history buffs will delight in these 24 terrifying tales, based on reportedly true accounts.

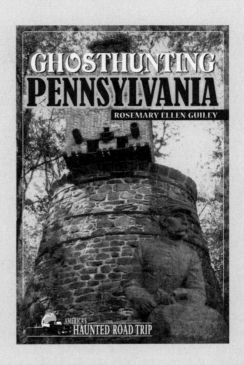

Ghosthunting Pennsylvania:
America's Haunted Road Trip

Rosemary Ellen Guiley

**ISBN: 978-1-57860-353-4 • $17.95 • 5.5 x 8.5
paperback • 224 pages**

One of the most respected paranormal investigators in the country, Rosemary Ellen Guiley leads you to 30 haunted places—all of which are open to the public—so you can test your own ghosthunting skills. Join Rosemary as she explores each site, snooping around eerie rooms and dark corners, talking to people who swear to their paranormal experiences. Each entry includes a detailed description and photographs.

The Story of AdventureKEEN

We are an independent nature and outdoor activity publisher. Our founding dates back more than 40 years, guided then and now by our love of being in the woods and on the water, by our passion for reading and books, and by the sense of wonder and discovery made possible by spending time recreating outdoors in beautiful places.

It is our mission to share that wonder and fun with our readers, especially with those who haven't yet experienced all the physical and mental health benefits that nature and outdoor activity can bring.

#bewellbeoutdoors